The Resurrectionists

PRAISE FOR MICHAEL PATRICK HICKS

<u>BROKEN SHELLS</u>

"A fun and nasty little novella...If you're a big creature-feature fan (digging on works like Adam Cesare's *Video Night* or Hunter Shea's *They Rise*) you're going to love this book."
— Glenn Rolfe, author of *Becoming* and *Blood and Rain*

"An adrenaline-fueled, no punches pulled, onslaught of gruesome action! Highly recommended!"
— Horror After Dark

"Lightning fast...high octane fun."
— Unnerving Magazine

"*Broken Shells* is a blood-soaked, tense novella that is sure to appeal to a wide variety of horror fans, especially those that dig an old-school feel in their novels."
— The Horror Bookshelf

"The very definition of a page-turner. Michael Patrick Hicks delivers right-between-the-eyes terror."
— The Haunted Reading Room

"Unnerving! ... It truly is the perfect blend of gore, horror and action."
— PopHorror.com

"Michael Patrick Hicks has managed, in only 120 pages, to craft a terrifying, steamroller of a story. The author makes you immediately connect with the main character Antoine, who is down on his luck and just looking for a possible break. When Antoine is thrust into the dark, you are along for the ride, whether you like it or not. And in the dark is where this story shines. Hicks makes you feel dread, like the walls are closing in as you read."
— One-Legged Reviews

"Hicks does a fine job of emotionally grasping the reader with his character creation. You'll come for the story of survival, and stay for the darkness and gore. If you enjoy extremely gruesome creature horror and pitch black underground tunnels, then *Broken Shells* is right up your alley."

— FanFiAddict

MASS HYSTERIA

"Brutal horror. Raw. Animalistic. I couldn't put it down!"
— Armand Rosamilia, author of the Dying Days series

"*Mass Hysteria* is a hell of a brutal, end of the world free for all. A terrifying vision of a future gone mad with bloodlust, *Mass Hysteria* will haunt your nightmares."
— Hunter Shea, author of *Creature* and *We Are Always Watching*

"A mindfuck of a story masquerading as an apocalyptic thriller. Once it takes its mask off, it's *Night of the Comet* meets *Pink Flamingos*."
— Chris Sorensen, author of *The Nightmare Room*

"There are horror novels, and then there are HORROR novels. You know, the ones with blood dripping off the letters (and pages) and sinking deep into the pit of your soul, causing you to question the decency of humanity and existence itself. *Mass Hysteria*, by Michael Patrick Hicks, certainly falls into this latter category. Masterful storytelling, but NOT for the faint of heart. You've been warned."
— The Behrg, author of *Housebroken* and The Creation series

"Fun, horrible fun, from start to finish."
— Horror Novel Reviews

"It's fast paced, action-packed, and bloody. Really, almost everything a horror gore-hound could want. ... Undeniably talented, Michael Patrick Hicks shows evidence of a rather deliciously depraved mind..."

— SciFi & Scary

"*Mass Hysteria* was a brutal horror novel, which reminded me of the horror being written in the late 70's and, (all of the), 80's. Books like James Herbert's *The Rats* or Guy N. Smith's *The Night of the Crabs*. There are a lot of similarities to those classics here-the fast paced action going from scene to scene-with many gory deaths and other sick events. In fact, I think *Mass Hysteria* beats out those books in its sheer horrific brutality."

— Char's Horror Corner

"I'm telling you now, this book isn't for readers with weak stomachs. It is brutal in all the right ways."

— Cedar Hollow Horror Reviews

"If you are an aficionado of author Richard Laymon, you undoubtedly will like this book. This is horror at its bloodiest, guttiest and most shocking."

— Cheryl Stout, Amazon Top Reviewer

ALSO BY MICHAEL PATRICK HICKS

THE SALEM HAWLEY SERIES
The Resurrectionists (Book 1)

DRMR SERIES
Convergence (A DRMR Novel, Book 1)
Emergence (A DRMR Novel, Book 2)
Preservation (A DRMR Short Story)

OTHER NOVELS
Broken Shells: A Subterranean Horror Novella
Mass Hysteria

SHORT STORIES
The Marque
Black Site
Let Go
Revolver
Consumption

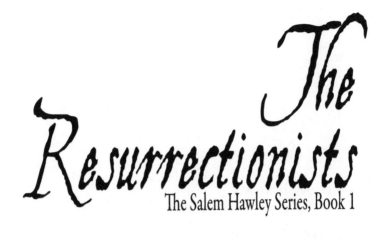

The Resurrectionists

The Salem Hawley Series, Book 1

Michael Patrick Hicks

To my wife and kids, always.

Chapter 1

The young woman's stays, its bindings cut with a surgeon's scalpel, sat in a heap on the floor. Her gauzy dress had been tossed aside. Eyes closed, she lay atop the table. Thick leather straps secured her wrists and feet to either end. Her dark scarlet hair hung in loose, springy curls around her face. The wound to her head and the blood that had issued forth from her scalp were hidden beneath the sprightly mound.

Her name was unimportant to the man standing over her. Her profession was equally irrelevant, as was the means by which she had been procured. Jonathan Hereford had paid twelve dollars to the team of resurrectionists he routinely hired to bring him bodies. Whether the bodies were living or deceased when the resurrectionists procured them typically made little difference to him, as the end result for the bodies was the same. However, some occasions dictated that the subject be delivered alive and in sufficiently good health.

The woman's eyelids fluttered, chasing consciousness like a moth to an evening light. In the flickering candlelight illuminating the room, one eye twitched open, followed slowly by the other. Her mouth tried to form words around a wooden bite block, then as the sight of the figure before her crystallized, she tried to scream. Her teeth and mouth worked furiously to dislodge the bite block, already well-scored by dozens of sets of teeth, but the hunk of wood was wedged tightly, affixed to her straining, shaking head by leather straps buckled behind her skull. Spit leaked from the corners of her mouth, staining the wet wood black.

Her eyes were opened wide in disbelief, and her freckled face contorted with fear, her lips pinching against the bite block as her nostrils flared, her breathing hitching through her nose in a loud, windy panic. A slender man draped in a thick, waxed overcoat stood over her, his hands gloved in shiny black leather to match the coat. His face was hidden behind a large-beaked mask. She shook her head in violent denial, the cords of her neck standing on end as she strained against her bonds. Hereford knew what she was seeing. He understood the fright she felt as she caught sight of her reflection in the black glass eyes on either side of the long, pointed beak. He saw similar reflections in the eyes of the masks around him. When her eyes finally found the blade, her bladder emptied.

Hereford said not a word. Ignoring her, he turned to his five similarly dressed companions standing opposite the operating table, half hidden in the shadows as the penumbra of candlelight failed to fully reach them.

"Begin," a soft voice directed.

Hereford tilted his head in acknowledgement of the command. Beneath the mask, he smiled.

Curiosity overcame the woman's fear, if only briefly, and she turned toward the voice. A tiny flicker of hope touched her eyes then fled immediately. The sight of the beaked masks, her supine form mirrored in each darkened eye lens, was enough to rekindle her horror. The five plague doctors stepped fully in the light, encircling her. Their faces leaned in, cocked slightly, birdlike, to take in the death of her hope and relish the fright that seized her. Her screams were muffled by the bite block as she, again, tried to free her arms and legs, but the straps stuck her fast to the table. Hopelessness washed through her as the gallery of birdmen watched her choke back her sobs. One figure leaned in closer, nearly beak to nose with her, and she could almost see past her reflection in the darkly tinted glass of the eyepiece, but what she saw only quickened the pace of her nightmare. She caught a glimmer of a dark eye, hungry and lecherous.

Hereford savored the sight of the naked woman, his breath quickening as his penis lumbered to life. He studied her milky pale skin and the smattering of freckles across her face, chest, and limbs. Her nipples were such a soft pink that they nearly disappeared into the creamy complexion of the fatty mounds surrounding them. Her large breasts had fallen to either side of her ribs, and his eyes followed the doughy curve of her belly down to the deep triangular patch of bright-red hair between her shapely thighs. Behind the mask, he smiled in anticipation.

She fought against the restraints, thick ropes of saliva trailing down from the bite block to pool at her neck. He did not need to understand the words to know she was urgently begging him. Her heart would be racing, he knew, the blood pounding through her veins to create a thunderous pulse. Even through the oiled leather, he could feel the maniacal pumping of her heart as he pressed his palm to her sweat-slickened chest. Behind the mask, Hereford smiled and breathed deeply, inhaling the scent of lemon and herbs housed in the beak. His groin ached for release.

He pressed the scalpel to her chest, the blade biting into skin just beneath the hollow of her throat. In one fluid motion, he cut a clean straight line down to her pubis. The woman fought harder, her screaming louder and pained. He had opened the flesh down to the muscle. Her body needed a moment to understand what had happened, then blood began to pool in the wound and overflow the edges of the fresh trench, sheeting across her torso. He made a second, deeper pass to cut through the muscle.

Her head lurched off the table, her teeth embedded in the wooden block. She howled around it, red-faced and soaked in sweat.

Hereford's fingers dug into the narrow wound, widening the gap as he stretched apart the woman's flesh. Her skull crashed onto the tabletop, and she went still once more. He wondered if she had knocked herself unconscious or merely passed out from the extraordinary pain. He pried away the meat from her sternum, exposing the bone, and then reached for his chisel and hammer. He made several solid blows down the length of bone, cracking open her chest, then inserted a metal hinge stained a ruddy brown from old blood. He cranked it so that the jaws spread her ribs wide with a rusty squeal.

Inside her chest cavity beat her purple heart. The organ was a frenetic muscle, chaos and fury bound into beating purpose. As the tissues on either side flexed, the heart bounced within its thin pericardial sac, jangling with wild intent around the space afforded it within the mediastinum. It was rhythmic and beautiful, a perfect organic machine. It jogged insanely, like a hare driven mad with fear and seeking escape from the butcher's block.

He cut swiftly, severing the organ from its roots within the thoracic compartment. His gloved fingers slid beneath the heart as it slowed and pumped its last, then he pulled it free. Few things in life, he had discovered, were as satisfying as holding a human heart in one's own hand, and it sent a ripple of pleasure through him.

"Quickly now," a soft voice demanded.

The beaked doctor turned swiftly to the laboratory table behind him, where he placed the heart in a metal construct. Wires led from the small vertical cage to a nearby voltaic pile. He twisted a knob on the cage to push a pair of small metal disks into place on either side of the heart, completing the electric circuit. The muscles of the organ twitched and jiggered, forcing unenthusiastic gouts of blood trapped within the heart's chambers from the shortened arteries.

"It works," a woman said, sotto voce.

The beaked doctors exchanged glances in turn, some nervous, others broiling with excitement. All eyes turned toward Dr. Richard Bayley as they waited his final judgment. At last, he said, "We can begin."

Chapter 2

S wine, sent out the previous night to devour the trash left behind by thirty thousand illiterates, clogged the dirt streets of Manhattan. The loud-mouthed barkers selling slaves along the riverfront broke the early-morning quiet.

Maneuvering past cows and goats, Hereford marched down Broadway to New York Hospital. His every footstep was a noisy squelch through a churned slush of mud—and worse. Hereford had a day of lecturing medical apprentices on the subject of anatomy ahead of him. His enterprising students would have no doubt procured the necessary bodies for their lesson, and his face wrapped in a thick woolen scarf to keep the biting cold air at bay, he mentally prepared the notes for today's topic as he walked.

Lurking at the back of his mind, though, was the sight of a human heart slowly beating, throbbing, outside its female host. The dark early-morning hours had been wondrous, and he could not shake the image of the woman's heart installed in a metal cage, arcs of electricity encircling it and revivifying it. Such a vision was beyond glorious, and it instilled in him, as well as his fellow beak-masked surgeons, much hope for their future prospects.

Once her remains were no longer necessary for their ceremony, the woman Hereford had operated upon had been broken down through a rigorous routine of dismemberment by the accompanying plague doctors. Saws and blades were applied to the joints of her legs and arms as the surgeons operated in tandem to take apart the useless body and wrap the removed segments in cotton before they were placed in bags for disposal. Although cadavers for medical study were at a premium, Bayley was adamant that their professional standards be kept separate from their extracurricular experiments, allowing them to maintain a measure of purity in both. Hereford couldn't help but find it a touch superstitious, and he had argued as much before their small committee, only to be overruled.

Hereford had retreated to his apartment for sleep before his morning lecture, and by the time he arrived at the hospital, the woman would be scattered across the small island of Manhattan, her limbs sunk in the harbor or donated to the pigs for their morning sup. Some parts of her would discreetly be sold to soap boilers and tallow chandlers, her uses for science exhausted while several avenues for commerce remained. Those auctioned fatty segments would make for fine bars of soap or candlesticks. More than likely, Hereford thought, she was more useful in death than she had been in life.

Walking through the thick, icy slop, he rubbed at his burning, tired eyes. Although he had slept, it had not been untroubled. More than a decade after the war, the bleating screams of tortured men and musket fire too close for comfort still woke him easily and with troubling frequency. An hour of sleep, at best, was all he had been afforded, and it seemed that nearly as soon as he had shut his eyes, they had snapped open once more. The lingering noise still echoed in his ears—grown men howling around a bite block as the amputation of various limbs reduced them to a malodorous, infantile state.

Hereford had trained in London prior to his arrival in the young colonies. The war, however, had truly made him a doctor—and something other than a doctor as well. He recalled quite clearly rushing onto the battlefield of Camden, feeling the birth of something new and revelatory within himself, even among the field of so many dead.

Sweat pouring down his face in the extreme August heat, the air tinged with gun smoke and blood, he strode through the field, surrounded by pained moaning. The British had marched through the night. Just after dawn, they had met the advancing regiment of Americans, many of whom were sick from dysentery or beset by the heat. The British had struck first, killing a number of Virginia militiamen before launching a bayonet charge. Almost immediately, the militia was sent scrambling into retreat, taking the American commander, Major-General Horatio Gates, into flight with them.

The coward, Hereford thought.

After less than an hour of fighting, a thousand

Americans were left dead and wounded, with another thousand taken captive.

Blood soaked the field, and flies were already gathering in droves over the carcasses, landing upon men too wounded to shoo them away. A susurrating, buzzing cloud maneuvered through the fog hanging over the field, traveling from host to host, seeking nourishment.

Attracted by the sweat pouring off him, the deafening cloud encircled Hereford's head as he cut a path through the killing field. He breathed through his mouth, one hand held to his face in an effort to keep the flies and the stench of fresh shit at bay. All night, the men had been shitting bloody water, holding their bellies, and complaining of aches and fevers. For many, the British succeeded where the dysentery failed. Those who had been praying for death the night prior had their dark wishes answered on an August dawn.

Clothes sweat-glued to his body, Hereford stepped between the bodies, sorting the living from the dead as he passed. For some, it required no more than a mere glance to determine if they were animate. For others, their state of being was immediately apparent. Scores upon scores had been run through with bayonets, killed during close-quarters combat when British forces charged the right wing, assaulting the remnants of a militia already decimated by the redcoats' opening volley. Those who had not retreated were slaughtered, a task made all the easier for the British as the Virginians lacked both bayonets and adequate training. Others had taken musket balls to their vital organs, with steel shot through their heads, hearts, or throats. And others still had been felled by muskets then pierced by blades to finish them off.

Maneuvering through the grisly scene, he directed his assistants to separate the wounded. Through dark clouds of flies, he saw a second ephemeral form, distinct in its own right, darker and wispier than those of the carrion insects. Flitting through the air, it would find and settle atop a corpse, like an illicit lover taking the men into its embrace and sliding over their torsos. Needles of black vapor curled into split lips and threaded its way up the nostrils, enshrouding the individual's head in a constantly stirring sack of mist.

Hereford stood stock-still, his pulse racing, flies alighting along his gore-slicked arms. Over the last four years of fighting, of rushing onto battlefields to haul away maimed, writhing bodies, he had learned fear and developed a keen appreciation for the body's natural instincts. He had come to know what it was like to live perpetually afraid. Yet the fear he felt in that moment was unlike any he had felt previously. Even as cannons and muskets fired and men fought to death in melee combat, fighting with bayonets and knives and swords, he had still found the will to move. With this unnatural mist shifting across the fallen, Hereford found his legs unresponsive, his tense spine glued straight. His mouth had gone dry, his tongue thick and heavy as it sat in a hollow cave of parchment. Despite the extraordinary heat, his teeth chattered, and he wished his legs could gallop as forcefully as his heart pummeled his breastbone.

Tendrils stretched away from the mist, unnaturally long and quite nearly transparent in its thinness. After a moment of study, Hereford recognized them as arms—first two, then four, five, and six of them seeking the edges of the body the otherwise-formless shape had attached itself to and reaching out to explore the neighboring bodies.

To the left of the fog was a wounded Virginian, his hands pressed tightly to his belly. Hereford could make out the purplish bulge of intestine pushing forth between the man's bloodied fingers. Head arched back, the veins on either side of his neck protruding, his struggling face a rictus of pain, the man screamed loudly—the surest sign of life Hereford had ever seen.

As the mist encountered the wounded man, his screams grew louder and panicked. His heels kicked uselessly at the ground, pushing through earth sodden with bodily fluids. Flowing from the corpse and onto the wounded man, the black fog enshrouded him fully, wrapping tendrils around the man's thick neck as if to choke him. Fingerlike lengths of mist floated over the man's chin, sneaking into his mouth.

Hereford watched in morbid fascination as the Virginian's screams sputtered into garbled chokes and his face empurpled beneath the shifting, translucent darkness. As his head arched farther back, the bulge of viscera peeping from between his fingers plopped forward. His hands fell away as intestines burst forth from the wound. Steam rose from the man's mouth and curled into the air, drifting several inches above him before becoming lost to the sky. Then, his gagging finished, his arched back settled into the bloodied mud, and his head sank to the side. The mist lingered, creating small traceries of black smoke pulled from the man's nostrils—what Hereford initially understood to be his dying breath. Then the body was perfectly still. The mist came alive, slinking off the expired soldier, and inched its way toward another one of the felled militiamen.

Revolted, but also deeply curious, Hereford studied the black smoke as it fed off the third body. When a fly landed on his tongue, he realized he was standing with his mouth agape in equal measures of wonder and horror. With his arm, he swiped at the sweat sheeting down his forehead, instantly turning his sleeve sodden and black with moisture.

"Do you see this?" he asked, turning toward an assistant. But the other man was gone, carting a body downfield toward the medical tent. Nobody living was near to answer him, and the absolute loneliness of his predicament crashed upon him. He stood alone in a field of the dead, inhaling fecund air ghastly enough to taste. He looked back toward the roiling black fog in time to see it stretch into the air above a fresh corpse, fanning out and dissipating until it was lost fully to the sky.

After several moments, Hereford collected his wits. Shaken, his nerves wrecked by the mystery he had witnessed, he was eager to return to his duties nonetheless. A number of patients still awaited triage. And perhaps, if they could not be saved, their deaths could yet summon the oddity for further inspection.

New York Hospital rose in the distance as a cold wind whipped across Hereford's face, violently pulling him away from his decade-old thoughts. He had not seen that sentient, animate fog again, but its possible presence was never far from his mind, particularly during surgeries when the veil between life and death was razor thin. And although he had not seen it himself, he had heard tell of the fog's arrival elsewhere and in different forms.

Several of his fellow medical practitioners had spoken in hushed whispers of strange sights during the war, when acres of farmland had been turned into killing fields and gravesites heady with the stench of blood that lured forth impossible abominations. To some, it appeared as a mist similar to what Hereford had seen. To others, the dying were preyed upon by slick-looking, featureless creatures blacker than a starless night, their long-limbed forms mounting their victims to inhale soldiers' dying breaths.

He'd never seen anything matching the latter

description, but he hoped to satisfy his curiosity one day. He hoped, too, that the evening activities he took part in with the small group of doctors who formed the hospital's secret inner circle of physicians might yet lure forth such anomalies. That was the end goal, or one of them, at least. Hereford was not a Christian, but he had seen enough of life and death to believe in the beyond and whatever may exist between this world and the next. As men and women of science, they sought answers, and the secrets to so many of life's mysteries could only be divined in the study of death.

Approaching the hospital entrance, he couldn't help but think of the redheaded corpse their small group had studied the previous night. Hereford had examined her exactingly as she lay unconscious and bound to the operating table, committing as much detail as he could to memory. A warmth grew in his crotch, even as he forced aside the alluring mental imagery of her luscious thighs and the pliability of her flesh as his fingers sank into her skin.

They had been unable to summon forth life from the void, but not for want of trying. As he opened the door and stepped into the hospital, he could still hear the sizzle of blood from her heart frying as electricity struck it. Scientific studies such as theirs needed to be rigorous, thorough, and required extensive experimentation. Last night's experiment had not been successful, but it had not been an utter failure, either. They would try again and again and again, for as long as it took.

Chapter 3

Prince's printing had grown stronger, even if the lines he drew were unsure, ill-formed, and oddly slanted on the paper. But he was learning, and that was the important part. Salem Hawley ran the eight-year-old through another round of the alphabet, making him write out the twenty-six letters in capitals and their lowercase counterparts.

"That's good!" Hawley said, admiring the child's chicken scratch. He couldn't help but smile. The letters were small and grouped tightly together, which Hawley understood to be a representation of the child's shy, quiet personality. Over the past few months, the letters had at least gotten larger and bolder, as had Prince's esteem. Knowledge was power, and the boy was quickly learning he was stronger than he gave himself credit for.

They spent time working on Prince's numbers—he could count to five with little trouble but needed some extra encouragement and gentle reminding to hit the first double-digit number. After a few cycles of counting, the time came for the boy to tend to his afternoon chores and clean out the chicken coop.

Warming Hawley's heart before the cold outside froze his body, Prince wrapped his arms around Hawley's waist and gave him a tight hug. "Thank you, Mr. Hawley."

"You did good today, Prince. I shall see you tomorrow." After slipping on his leather overcoat and encircling his face with a scarf, Hawley donned a hat and made his way out of the house, hands buried deeply in his pockets. The air was biting viciously, and strong winds lashed at his skin with a whip-crack sharpness, a feeling Hawley recalled all too easily. Sheets of snow blasted into his face, stinging his eyes.

Pigs grunting caught his attention, and he frowned in dismay at the sight. The barrel-shaped animals were covered in filth, their hooves buried in sewage, their snorting nostrils nearly inhaling the wretched muck as they fought over their treasure. As their rotund bodies shifted, Hawley caught sight of curled fingers and a stretch of gray forearm that terminated at the elbow joint. The swine had torn away chunks of flesh, leaving jagged, bloodless holes devoured down to the bone. One jockeyed its way between the others and seized several fingers with a biting crunch, snapping them loose with a self-indulgent wag of its curly tail.

"Damnable beasts," Hawley muttered to himself, carrying on his way. He shook his head ruefully, cheeks burning beneath his wool coverings.

Earlier in the month, he and a number of the city's other free blacks had attended a council meeting to petition for the end of desecration to the Negroes Burial Grounds. The potter's field had been routinely looted by medical students in need of bodies for their anatomy lessons and dissections. The city's night watch did little to prevent it, focusing their efforts on protecting the white cemeteries. Meanwhile, Negro burial plots were ransacked by teams of resurrectionists, the corpses of friends and family stolen away in the darkest hours of night. Their hacked-apart remains were scattered around the filthy island for the pigs to feast on and for birds to pick at.

Acid boiled in Hawley's stomach, his blood up and nerves rankled. The heat of anger was a welcome distraction from the February freeze, and with some surprise, he found himself banging harshly up the steps to his apartment with little recollection of the trip that had brought him there. Gluttonous pigs and the dark thoughts of body snatchers were the last thing he truly recalled before his mind slipped away in a fog.

A small chortle escaped his throat, and he removed his hat, beating it against his leg to knock off the snow. He reached the landing to the third floor and maneuvered down a creaking hallway to his small room. The womenfolk were busy cooking their men meals for the afternoon, and a variety of African spices tinged the air. Everything from jerk to cinnamon, with dashes of cardamom, ginger, and harissa, mingled with the smells of boiling goat meat and veal. Voices echoed above the odors, a litany of accents, dialects, and languages, each distinct from another. The apartment complex housed Africans, Caribbean islanders, and more, all freed during the war, their freedom either bought or won.

Thanks to the thin walls, closing the apartment door behind him did little to minimize the noise of his neighbors, but the delightful smells from their kitchens were certainly welcome. His outerwear shed and hung to dry, Hawley set about warming the kettle for tea while he carved off a thick chunk of bread and squares of salted meat to lunch upon.

A banging on his door interrupted his meal. A deeply stentorian voice shouted, "Salem! You in there?"

Chair scraping against the wooden planks, Hawley stood, taking one last bite of meat and bread, then wiped his hands against the thighs of his pants. He opened the door to a tear-streaked face in time to see the man swipe away snot from his upper lip with the back of his hand.

"Jeremiah? Good God, man." Hawley stepped back to let the disheveled man inside. Jeremiah had lost his wife and infant days ago, the former shuffling off her mortal coil in the failed delivery of the latter. In the span of mere hours, Jeremiah lost all he held dear in the world. He stood before Hawley, a hollowed man. The once square-shouldered figure now stooped with the weight of tragedy, his wet and tired eyes red and sunken atop thick purple bags that hung over cracked, downturned lips.

"They took them," Jeremiah shouted, pacing the length of the small living area. Boards creaked beneath every footstep.

"Who?" Hawley asked, fearing he already knew the answer. His friend's words bowed his head, and his heart sank into his belly, sickened.

"Nina and Juliet. They're gone, both of them."

The woman and her child had been buried together in the potter's field at the end of Chambers Street, not far from New York Hospital. Hawley recalled the sight of the small infant swaddled in a bundle of stained white cloths, the mother's arms crossed over the baby and clutching the child to her breast.

"They didn't even try to hide what they done," Jeremiah said. "The ground was all busted up, their coffin broken apart." He tried to speak more, but his words were reduced to blubbering sobs. His fingers pinched the bridge of his nose in a failed attempt to stem the flood of tears.

Hawley put an arm around the taller man's shoulders and guided him into the lone chair at the small kitchen table. Hawley took the whistling kettle off the fire and poured them each a cup of tea. He couldn't shake the sight of those pigs tearing into the severed arm in the street, snow falling against ashen skin, nothing but bright white and deep red wounds against the mud. He leaned against the counter and took a tentative sip, blowing softly over the edge of the cup to cool the liquid inside.

"What can I do?" Hawley asked, sure that Jeremiah had some idea on how to correct the injustice. Jeremiah had led the failed petition to the council before Nina's and Juliet's passing.

"You're the letters man," Jeremiah began. "Would you be willing to write a letter?"

"I would, if you think it will help."

"It wouldn't be going to the council."

"Who then?"

"Francis Childs," Jeremiah said.

Hawley nodded. The name was familiar to him. Childs was the editor and publisher of the *New York Daily Advertiser*. He was also anti-slavery, and while that fact did not immediately make the white man an ally, he would perhaps be more sympathetic to their plight than the city council would. It might even rile up some of his readers.

"I will begin immediately."

"I want your help tonight as well," Jeremiah said. "At the cemetery."

Hawley hid his rueful smile behind the cup of tea. Anger rose in him anew alongside the prospect of justice for Jeremiah and his family. Hawley was an accomplished man when he was angry, as both a scholar and a fighter, or at least he had been during the war. He found himself suddenly eager to see how true that still was. "Of course," he said.

Hawley spent the better part of the afternoon sitting before the fire, with a blanket over his shoulders to keep the cold air bleeding through the alley-side walls at bay as he drafted a letter to Childs. It needed to be concise but also emotionally appealing in its call to action toward an otherwise-indifferent crowd. He struggled to find an opening that would impart the gravity of the predicament facing the colored community and make the city pay attention to the abhorrent sacrilege they suffered.

As if whites ever gave a damn about the black community, Hawley thought bitterly, *beyond beating or killing us or selling us.* He could ill afford to waste ink on a rant that would only lose him more ears than it would ever gain, and he had to fight for a moment to clear his mind before he was finally ready to set pen to paper.

The repositories of the dead have been

> *held in a manner sacred, in all ages, and almost in all countries. It is a shame that they should be so very scandalously dealt with, as I have been informed they are in this City. It is said that few blacks are buried, whose bodies are permitted to remain in the grave.*

A calmness came over Hawley as he wrote. He felt as if he were finding his groove. The message of import seized him, commanding him, and the words poured forth.

> *Swine have been seen devouring the entrails and flesh of women! Human flesh has been taken up along the docks, sewed up in bags!*

Perhaps it was best not to dwell on the grislier aspects, he decided, still burdened with the grotesque imagery of pigs feasting on a woman's severed arm while chomping and snorting noisily as they jostled one another for a seat at the table. He shoved those thoughts aside, needing to focus on offering a solution. He had outlined the problem, sought to rile up those who would read this letter, and engaged his audience emotionally. Now he needed to give them an action, something concrete and resolute.

> *If a law was passed, prohibiting the bodies of any other than Criminals from being dissected, unless by particular desire of the dying for the benefit of mankind, a stop might be put to the horrid practice here; and the minds of a very great*

> *number of my fellow-liberated, or still enslaved Negroes, quieted. By publishing this, you will greatly oblige both them, and your very humble servant.*

He ended the letter with a flourish, using the pseudonym Humanio. Childs may have been anti-slavery, but Hawley knew better than to blindly trust a white man, and a stranger at that, let alone have his name published in a newspaper as well circulated as the *Advertiser*.

Presuming, that is, it becomes published, he admonished himself.

Childs spoke well and openly of his disbelief in the necessity of enslavement, but Hawley knew despite the effort of this composition to Childs, he could ignore the petition just as easily as the community council had. Besides, if Hawley put his own name out there, what would stop the resurrectionist bandits from employing live subjects such as him in their medical experiments?

No, Hawley decided, it was rather prudent to err on the side of caution.

"What do you think?" he said, handing the note to his friend.

Jeremiah scratched at the patchwork of scruff across his jaw as he read, pulling slightly at the thin growths of hair populating his chin. Fresh tears stood in small beads against the thin beard over his cheeks, and he wiped them away with his sleeve.

"They shouldn't get any bodies at all," Jeremiah nearly shouted. "What they're doing to those people is an abomination!"

Hawley nodded, although he had meant what he had written. He understood the necessity of cadavers for medical study and thought that perhaps a better education on the terms of the human body by practitioners would help advance the field of medicine. It might even have saved the lives of Juliet and Nina. Jeremiah, he knew, lacked any sort of disposition to hear such thoughts, and he dared not invoke the names of his departed beloveds. Instead, he merely waited for Jeremiah to cool.

"Do *you* think this is good?" Jeremiah asked, holding the paper between his two hands, his eyes intent on the words. His was an honest question, not a reprobation.

"I do," Hawley said.

Jeremiah studied the letter briefly before nodding and returning it to Hawley. "Fine then. We can drop it off this evening."

Hawley folded it into thirds and placed it into an envelope, which he scrawled Childs's name upon. "We shall reconvene this evening then, downstairs."

He wrapped his arms around Jeremiah's wide, muscular shoulders and patted him on the back. The man's warm tears moistened Hawley's cheeks.

"Lord, I miss her," Jeremiah said, choking the words out.

Hawley, who had already spent so much time over the last few days commiserating and telling his friend how awful it was and how sorry he was, did not know what else to say. He squeezed the man in his arms and said simply, "We'll get them. Whoever took them, we will not rest until justice is met."

The intervening hours were met with the sharpening

of a blade. Hawley ran the stone over the tomahawk's edge until he was satisfied with the weapon's sharpness. He prepared a fresh cup of tea, which he drank as time slipped past.

Both he and Jeremiah had performed scouting missions and reconnaissance during the war, typically during the night hours. Although their commander had initially been adamant that no Negro would serve in the colonial army, his superiors had made him relent. During the duration of their service, the commander had begun to realize how well a dark-skinned Negro such as Salem Hawley could be utilized. Silent, swift-moving, and with flesh the color of night, Hawley had often been dispatched ahead of his unit to spy on British placements and report back enemy numbers to the officers.

An odd sense of calmness had always enveloped Hawley during those missions. The evening he left his apartment to meet Jeremiah, he felt much the same—prepared and with the quietude of professionalism settling into his bones. The axe hung from his belt loop, the blade hidden beneath his coat.

Jeremiah followed him out the door a moment later, and their feet crunched through a fresh layer of snow. Together, they walked in silence, the sky above moonless.

At the small office of the *New York Daily Advertiser*, Hawley slipped the envelope to Childs between door and jamb. The thin letter slid easily into the building. Their faces wrapped in scarves, heads capped by brimmed hats, Hawley was certain that if anybody were watching neither he nor Jeremiah could be easily identified. The office was dark, though, as were the neighboring shops, and he doubted any eyes at all had alighted upon them.

The men continued on their way, following Chambers Street to its end then through uneven mud and slurries of churned earth, ice, and snow to the Negroes Burial Grounds.

"Fresh graves are this way," Jeremiah said.

Hawley followed, conscious of the tomahawk hidden at his waist.

Voices carried to them between strong gusts of wind over the plots of graves, the words indistinct. The two men dropped into a crouch, their feet light as they hurried quietly across the earth. Dim lanterns arranged around a burial plot revealed three resurrectionists breaking through freshly dug soil with wooden shovels. Two were in the process of opening a hole on either side of the grave marker, while the third kept watch, ignorant of Hawley and Jeremiah's approach.

Hawley slowly slid the tomahawk free, keeping his movements small as he tucked himself into the shadows. A flash of silver proved Jeremiah to be similarly armed.

A hollow tap announced the meeting of the wooden shovel blade with the pine box buried beneath them. As Hawley made his approach, a splintering crack rang out in the air, and the men moved quickly.

Hawley covered the distance between them as fast as he could, a mild horror shaking through him as one of the youthful white men dragged free from the earth a freshly dead Negro, arms hooked through the cadaver's arm pits. A companion moved in to help, laying the deceased out on the cold ground.

The crunch of a frozen clod of dirt popping drew the attention of the three men. Jeremiah darted forward, an inchoate scream of rage startling the body snatchers.

"Jeremiah, no!" Hawley said. But it was too late. Whatever plan of stealth and distraction they'd possessed was gone, dismissed completely and utterly by his friend's justified, yet ill-timed, outrage. And he'd given away his own position, drawing two of the grave robbers toward him.

The watcher was the quickest, and he snatched up a shovel, moving forward to meet Jeremiah head-on. As Jeremiah let a fist fly, the watcher dodged the blow and stepped into the opening his larger opponent had made. The end of the shovel's handle smashed into the underside of Jeremiah's jaw. The rattle of his teeth was harsh in the silent night. The man took a step back, raising the shovel, and swung hard. Wood collided with skull.

Hawley raised his tomahawk, careful not to put his back to either of the two men and to keep them both within his line of sight. They rushed him from either side. Hawley swung at the closest man and was rewarded with a surprised yelp of pain. But as he wounded one, the other closed in quick. When swung, the long shovel in his hand tidily closed the gap between them. Pain exploded along Hawley's flank, stealing the wind from him as he was driven to his knees. The shovel came around at him again, and this time, he was ready. He took the hit to his ribs then pinned the shaft beneath his arm. He swung the tomahawk again, but he lacked the reach. The resurrectionist easily dodged the blade then yanked the shovel blade loose, pulling Hawley to the ground. The injured grave robber seized the moment and darted in, delivering a swift kick to Hawley's belly. Then the man with the shovel joined in, and Hawley felt utterly helpless. That pained him more than the assault waged upon his body.

Jeremiah's screams were loud, louder than the unending noise of the flat side of the shovel's blade pummeling Hawley's legs and arms. In between his friend's wails, Hawley heard, too clearly, the fracturing of Jeremiah's bones. His friend's cries were lost beneath the rush of blood in Hawley's ears as his own attacker struck him with a shovel, raining down blow after blow along the backside of his body. From the other side, the points of a boot kicked into his ribs again and again. His tomahawk lost, Hawley curled into a ball, using his arms to protect his head, his eyes stinging. He cried in pain as much as shame.

"Come on!" one of the resurrectionists said.

Hawley hurt far too much to do anything besides watch as the trio gathered around the exhumed corpse and stripped it bare. The man's burial clothes were left in a heap beside the open pit, the cracked lid of his coffin left carelessly on the mound of dirt. One resurrectionist bent and hoisted the cadaver onto his shoulder, then they were off. Blood pounding in his ears, Hawley could make out none of their words, but he understood their peals of laughter against the moonless sky.

He dragged himself across the freezing ground to his old friend. Jeremiah had gone silent, his face a pulped, leaking wreck. Pulpy gray matter oozed from his shattered skull. Blood drained from his body and pooled atop frozen earth, the trodden snow surrounding him stained red.

Chapter 4

Hereford fished loose a cent for the street urchin hawking copies of *The Daily Advertiser*, then he jammed the folded sheet under his arm as he proceeded into a tavern. After a moment, his eyes adjusted from the fading sunlight to the candlelit interior, and he spotted a pair of familiar faces: Dr. Richard Bayley, his face softly lined with white hair hanging just past the tops of his ears, and his twenty-year-old protégé and son-in-law, Wright Post.

"Good evening, Jonathan," Dr. Bayley said.

"Richard, Wright." Hereford greeted them as he

folded his coat over the back of an empty chair, squaring his hat and scarf over the newspaper atop the table beside his seat.

"Have you read it?" Bayley asked, nodding toward the newspaper.

"I've only just bought it. Perhaps I'll save it to read over a brandy this evening."

"There's quite a letter in there, written by a Negro complaining about our studies of the physic."

"*Childs*," Post spat, the name of the newspaper's editor an epithet on his tongue. A New York native, Post did not share his father-in-law's London accent, despite the two years of study abroad undertaken at Hereford's insistence.

Hereford felt a twinge curling in his guts, well aware of where Bayley was directing the discussion.

"I understand some of your students had an encounter last night." Bayley sipped his ale, watching Hereford over the rim of his mug.

"Yes. John Hicks, Jr. and a few of his mates. I've spoken with him already."

"The boy is impudent," Bayley said.

"His youth gets the better of him," Hereford said. Hicks was a fifteen-year-old freshman and the son of a doctor who had served as a physician at General Hospital during the British Occupation several years previously.

Bayley, too, had been a Loyalist and served as a surgeon in the British Army, stationed in Rhode Island. His wife's illness and subsequent death little more than a decade prior had brought Bayley to New York. He had resigned and focused on his medical practice and treating the poor.

"See to it that it does not get the better of anyone else," Bayley said. "We have come too far and have much left to do."

The note of warning in Bayley's voice was unmistakable. Hereford was left with no recourse but to nod. He noticed that Bayley did not bother asking how badly wounded Hicks was, although in truth the injury was merely a trifle.

Hereford understood the older man's caution, even if he believed it to be unwarranted. Should the prior night's activities come to light, he doubted it would be difficult to make the young Hicks into something of a hero. The public would be easily convinced that the Negroes had been robbing their own dead and that, upon hearing the commotion, Hicks and his classmates had sought to halt the desecration of these graves. Most blacks were little more than illiterate criminals, and perhaps they had been stealing the corpses to sell on the black market. It would not take much to court public opinion in Hicks's favor. Even if most of that public itself was also illiterate and uneducated, they would trust a white man of means and money over an African savage, and the more salacious the crime, the easier it would be to sell.

Silence stretched briefly over the three men as a tavern maid set out bowls of stew and bread before them, along with a glass of wheat-colored ale for Hereford.

"Are the preparations for tonight completed?" Bayley asked.

Hereford studied the older man's face, nodding around a mouthful of potato and rich gravy. "They are."

The tavern was filled with noisy chatter and the occasional boisterous shouts, but the men leaned close, both to hear one another and to keep their conversation private.

"My associates will meet us at the hospital later this evening," Hereford said. "We can begin shortly thereafter."

"Excellent," Bayley said as his son-in-law offered a

wolfish smile.

Although Bayley had been a Loyalist and Hereford on the side of the Americans, their practice of medicine united them, as did the practice of older, more arcane activities and the witnessing of events that defied understanding of the natural state of affairs. Bayley had seen similar entities on the battlefield—flashes of unnatural smoke preying with odd devotion upon the dying.

Bayley had sought to reignite the interest of the creature—or creatures, as was perhaps more apt, in Hereford's opinion—by experimenting on captured wounded soldiers. He would cut into them with varying degrees of savagery and perform unnecessary amputations. One imprisoned colonial soldier had been reduced to little more than a torso, head, and a collection of stumps where all of his limbs had been methodically excised. The wounds had turned gangrenous, and as the fever consumed him, Bayley sought still to drive more agony into the man and rejuvenate the smoky spirit. He'd plucked the man's eyes from his skull, ripped loose the man's tongue, and peeled away his lips beneath a scalpel's edge. Some claimed that Bayley's experiments would have made the Christ-followers of the Spanish Inquisition seem tame in comparison. With no regard toward his conscious or immortal soul, Bayley eviscerated, maimed, mutilated, murdered, and burned scores of men in pursuit of a mystic sight, all the while proclaiming the advancement of the physic and the pursuit of study.

As Hereford became acquainted with Bayley during their lectures at New York Hospital, the men danced around their history and wartime accounts. By then, Hereford had heard many of the rumors that dogged Bayley, and he'd chalked much of it up to grandiose imagination of his young students and the gossiping of their less-proficient fellow lecturers. Then, after being steeled by much brandy and warmed by Bayley's company, he spoke for the first time to any living man of the formless, stygian creature he had witnessed several years prior. Bayley had listened patiently, his face betraying signs of neither skepticism nor even faint interest. Hereford drunkenly rambled, confessing of his own depraved experiments on wounded soldiers, his enthusiasm to inflict suffering driven by curiosity over the creature.

Bayley said nothing, and as Hereford's words died off, the weight of quietude settled between them. Then Bayley stood from his chair and silently left Hereford to his drunken stupor. Prior to his next lecture, Hereford arrived at the hospital to find Bayley waiting for him with an item wrapped in black cloth.

"What is this?" Hereford asked upon receiving the item from the good doctor.

"Read it," Bayley said. In his eyes lived a spark of encouragement, and as he stared at Hereford, the younger man felt the heaviness of scrutiny—and danger. "See me when you are finished. I believe we should talk more."

With that, Bayley again left him. Hereford's students began arriving, and he tucked the package away, forgetting about it until his return home later that evening. Sitting in the lantern glow of his parlor, brandy in hand, he unwrapped the silk cloth to reveal a leather book bound by a well-worn leather strap and secured by a metal clasp. There was no title on the front or along the spine, but a richly ornate frontispiece indicated the tome was titled *Al Azif,* authored by Abd al-Hazred.

The thin onionskin pages inside bore a litany of characters that Hereford could not discern, along with loose leaves of notes he recognized as Classical and Romantic languages. The book's spine was deformed by the bulge of added, unbound material, and as he thumbed through the collection of papers, he saw fragments of Greek, Latin, and French translations, all in distinctly different handwriting. Even the material, apparent age, and thickness of the additional pages varied. The tome itself smelled faintly of smoke, and he noticed streaks of ash across the rough uncut edges of paper, as well as dark copper spots dotting a number of the pages. He leafed through the book, examining the package as a whole, eventually finding snippets of English translations scattered throughout. Although he could read Latin easily enough, the English segments were far easier to discern.

One sheaf had been, seemingly, hastily torn. The handwritten English was sloppy and rushed, the ink smeared about the letters. He had noticed the couplet appear several times throughout *Al Azif,* mostly in Greek and Latin, but this was the first instance of its appearance in his own native tongue:

> *That is not dead which can eternal lie.*
> *And with strange aeons even death may die.*

A dark, foul sensation trickled down his spine. Hereford continued reading, the hairs along the back of his neck rising with the chill, his thighs damp and cool with sweat beneath the leather book pressing against his pants. The candle beside him flickered, sucking at the air with a breathy whoosh.

> *Nor is it to be thought that man is either the oldest or the last of earth's masters, or that the common bulk of life and substance walks alone. The Old Ones were, the Old Ones are, and the Old Ones shall be. Not in the spaces we know, but between them…*
> *They shall break through again. He knows where They had trod earth's fields, and where They still tread them, and why no one can behold Them as They tread. By Their smell can men sometimes know Them near, but of Their semblance can no man know, saving only in the features of those They have begotten on mankind; and of those are there many sorts, differing in likeness from man's truest eidolon to that shape without sight or substance which is Them.*

The Old Ones? he thought. A curious phrase, but more captivating was the semblance, or perhaps lack thereof, that such a creature displayed. Immediately, he recalled the ethereal figures lurking among the scores of bodies littering a bloodstained battlefield.

If the snatches of cursive ink he read weren't sinister enough, the accompanying imagery beneath the blackletter script was far more perverse. The illustrations were crude and depicted a number of tortuous scenarios. In some, women, pain clearly etched into their faces, were flayed alive, great swatches of skin peeled away to reveal the purple mess beneath. Others showed men whose skin bulged in disturbing provinces, as if the internal organs were seeking escape. Tentacles coiled around the human figures, ensnaring them in unnaturally long and barbed appendages that threaded through the bodies of men, women, and children. One image showed, with grotesque flair, a woman whose features were contorted in beautiful agony, her fingers dug deeply into the skin of her belly to pry apart the flesh, exposing her abdominal cavity. Inside was a fungal mass whose gossamer limbs slithered around various organs, ensnaring them in a mossy web. The foreign entity was all black eyes and toothy mouths, dozens of them across the surface of the eukaryotic creature.

A scream very nearly ejected from his mouth as he turned the page and came face-to-face with the bloodcurdling image of an ancient figure the author had identified as Baen'sollogotgartha. Thickly muscled, the gargantuan was a mass of long limbs and ropy feelers, its oversized mouth lurking behind a cage of bone and set beneath spiderlike eyes.

Hereford's unease grew deeper as he paged through the grimoire. The candle sputtered, flickered, then sparked back to life with a dull roar. He felt as if he were being watched, and a knot of panic bloomed within him. Succumbing to the sensation, he cast a look over his shoulder toward the darkened recesses of his house. He saw nothing. He swallowed but breathed somewhat easier. Even as he turned his attention back to the book, he swore he could feel the weight of scrutiny, the press of foreign eyes heavy upon his back. His clothes and the flesh beneath them suddenly felt quite ill-fitting.

Fire wheezed and crackled beside him, startling him, and he slammed the tome shut. As he stood, he felt a muscular lash slide swiftly across the back of his knees as it darted upward, between his legs. His scrotum shriveled at the sudden contact. He spun, nearly tripping over the blanket at his feet, his heart racing. He was alone, and yet his senses told him otherwise. The Old Ones were there, in his home, in the space between. And they were calling to him.

He snatched up the candle, spilling hot wax across the top of his hand in his haste, and whirled, aiming the light at the shadows as if he could forcefully repel the darkness. The dim illumination revealed nothing. Nothing at all. Slowly, his galloping heart grew restive as his body relaxed, the cold sweat that had broken out leaving him chilly.

You fool, he cursed. He wiped at the sweat along his brow, no longer feeling so superstitious or cowardly as he began to realize he was fully alone. His home, as it so often was, remained empty.

Completing the circuit around the room, ferreting out the shadows cohabitating his study, he made to exit the room and proceed to bed. As he passed his chair, though, his eyes fell upon *Al Azif* once again. The book was open and had fallen to a page depicting a familiar scene. He could tell immediately that the artist was not Abd al-Hazred, for the picture was of finer quality, its strokes more assured. The image detailed a cratered field of corpses, hundreds of them, thousands even. Limbs askew, the bodies were piled one atop another. Shadowy creatures lurked over the remains, feeding. In the center of it stood a solitary man, his mouth opened in wonder… and fear. Hereford recognized the improbability, the *impossibility*, of his own face there, and shaken, he snapped the book shut once more and hurriedly buckled the straps through the metal clasps.

Like a child, he retreated to his bedroom and the safety and surety of his blankets. Despite his exhaustion, he failed to sleep, intent on watching the shadows instead. His mind raced, unwilling and unable to slow as a hundred thousand questions occupied his focus.

Fear and excitement intermingled, and he knew he *must* speak with Bayley forthwith.

The following morning, he steeled himself as his knuckles rapped upon the front door of Bayley's home, the thick grimoire clutched between his opposite arm and rib cage.

"Thinnies," Bayley said once Hereford had unloaded upon him the prior evening's events.

Blowing across the top of his teacup, Hereford arched his eyebrows in confusion. "Pardon?"

"Thinnies," Bayley said again, his meaning still quite unclear to the lost and bewildered Hereford.

Bayley sipped tea, casting a glance toward the study's entrance. The doors were still closed, and his new wife, Charlotte, had gone into the city. "The spaces in between," he said. "The barriers that separate us from the Old Ones. They are very thin, these metaphysical walls, and yet they keep at bay entire dimensions, whole worlds, and the gods themselves. They can be eroded, though… or torn down altogether."

Hereford blanched, his hand shaking and rattling the china he held, nearly spilling the tea upon the floor. "You're saying one of these… these 'thinnies' are in my home?"

Bayley chuckled, a good-natured growl. "You must expand your mind, my good doctor. No, the thinnies are not in your home. Or at least not in the way you suspect. Rather, they are everywhere, sir, *everywhere*. The gods have turned their attention toward us once more. We have made them take notice, I suspect."

"How so?" Hereford asked.

"They are capricious, violent beasts, much like mankind itself. We have baited the water with fresh blood and drawn their attention. Now they will return to take back what is rightfully theirs."

"How do we stop them?" Hereford asked immediately.

Bayley stood, settling his teacup on the table beside his wingback chair. He put his hands on either of his companion's shoulders, demanding the doctor look up toward him to meet his eyes. "We do not. We cannot. They have revealed themselves to you and me—and a few others, I admit—and it is time to embrace their notice. We serve them. We *must* serve them."

Hereford struggled to retain his calm. Bayley's eyes were wide and wild, fevered with the burning fire of a true believer. Hereford himself was a believer. Regardless of how strongly his rational mind protested the acceptance of and acquiescence toward such insanity, after the preceding night, how could he not believe? He had been touched—and touched in his most private of areas, at that—by the mystical, otherworldly Old Ones. He had borne witness to the impossible, first in the aftermath of battle and again in his own study the prior night, and it had sought him in return.

With one shaking hand, Hereford raised the tea to his lips and drank. After a deep breath, he willed himself to meet Bayley's eyes once more, the older man standing above him still.

"How do we help them?" he asked.

A slow smile crossed Bayley's lips, and his eyes closed as he knelt closer, and in a strangely intimate gesture, he pressed his forehead to Hereford's. He rested his head against his companion's for a long moment, as if savoring the company, before speaking again. "Blood. Blood draws them forth. And death."

"Yes," Hereford whispered, recalling his time as a battlefield medic. He could remember with diamond clarity the stench of dead men, the swampy, oppressive heat tanged by blood and offal. He could hear the men scream, bite blocks clenched between their teeth, as jagged saws pulped flesh and bit into bone. He watched a man's blood soak a stained tourniquet, his own erection growing as he operated upon the soldier, willing the black velvet fog to embrace the struggling, wounded man.

"This war for independence," Bayley began, "and the sins that have built this foundling nation have a toll. Always, there is a toll. So, so much blood was loosed upon the earth. Between your wars and your slavers' whips, this infantile nation breeds blood and begets violence. It was ignorant to think such a thing could go unnoticed. We laid out a buffet, and Old Ones ate and ate, and we left them starved for more. They are here, and they are demanding."

"These thinnies," Hereford said. "They are more like doors than walls, then?"

Bayley nodded. "We must open them."

"How?"

"Suffering," Bayley said, as if it were obvious. "Suffering is always the key."

Burke and Moreland were late. After nearly half an hour, Bayley and Post began to grow impatient.

"Where are they?" Post complained.

"They'll be here," Hereford assured them. He had been working with the two resurrectionists for nearly a year, and they had performed well in the past.

"They must've caught a live one," Hicks said, with the usual impertinence of his youth and a gleaming smile set upon his wet lips.

Bayley shot the boy a look, bristling at the young man's cocky impishness, and bristling even further as John Hicks, Jr. smirked in return. Bayley's gloved hands curled into fists. Hereford put a hand on the older man's shoulder, encouraging him to remain calm. Then he pointed away from the hospital, toward a well-worn path and the hint of movement in the stygian darkness.

"There," he said, and Bayley followed the length of Hereford's pointing finger.

"Well, it's about time." Bayley sighed heavily, adjusting his thick black outer coat against the wind. After a moment, as if thinking better of continuing to linger in the cold, he turned on his heels and strode back into New York Hospital.

The hospital had housed British troops throughout the war for independence but had sat vacant since their surrender of New York. Much of the building was in disrepair, with only Bayley, Post, Hereford, and a few others occupying it with any degree of regularity to deliver their lectures to students of the physic.

Hicks breathed into his cupped hands, warming them with the hot air he was so fond of perniciously blowing. He gingerly danced from foot to foot, his cheeks, nose, and ears a bright scarlet. "Jay-sus! Could they walk the least bit slower?"

Hereford ignored him, even as the shared laughter from Burke and Moreland reached them. He wondered if they had heard Hicks's complaining and were perhaps lollygagging in an effort to further irritate the man-child. If they wanted Hicks's animus, they were welcome to it. Should they become too much of a bother for Bayley and a few other members of their small, tight circle… well, that was not likely to end well for Burke and Moreland. Both men were apt to spill their lifeblood through razor-slit throats in a darkened alley.

The resurrectionists took their time, but as they neared, Hereford could begin making out the bundle the larger man carried over his shoulder. Burke's arm was wrapped around a pair of long, slender legs clothed in torn hosiery, his fingers pressed into a shapely thigh just beneath the nicely rounded mound of the woman's skirted rump. Hereford could not discern any other features beyond leg and ass, but he still felt a familiar stirring at the approaching display.

The woman, he knew, was another one of the city's many prostitutes. Burke and Moreland often found such subjects when a living body was demanded of them, and they had proved themselves capable of meeting whatever Hereford demanded, corpses or otherwise.

"Take her," Hereford said, grabbing Hicks by the arm and shoving him toward the resurrectionists. As the boy took possession of the woman, Hereford reached into his trousers to fish out payment. In the moonlight, he caught sight of long brunette hair and a round, puckish face. She had pretty lips and high cheekbones. A lovely specimen, indeed.

Burke and Moreland stomped away, back into the cover of night. Hereford retrieved his medical bag from the ground and turned into the hospital. Hicks followed, grunting beneath the load.

The men traced a long, candlelit corridor that terminated at the entrance to the hospital's surgical auditorium. Hereford entered first, holding the door for his protégé.

Encircling the operating table were four figures hidden beneath thick leather coats and beaked masks. He set his medical bag upon a nearby table and undid the clasps. He withdrew two metal cages and stationed them in close proximity atop the table. Then he removed a voltaic pile and ran the wires about the cages, punching their ends into the muscle of the heart within each cage. He squeezed a sponge wet with salty brine over each heart. The fluid would provide the dry meat with the necessary conductivity for the flow of electricity. The hearts leapt to life, their chambers beating as if alive once more, and the sound of the animated muscles filled the operating room with a staccato noise.

Satisfied, he moved to the second table and readied himself for the ceremony to come. Hicks stood beside him, already in the process of drawing his ankle-length oilcloth cloak over himself. The woman had been arranged atop the operating table, and four plague doctors stood around her, their staffs in hand.

Hereford's flesh goose pimpled beneath the cold air, and he dressed quickly. The beak mask slid easily over his head and face, as if welcoming him, and he pushed aside the pretenses of his profession to better embrace the reality of his self. He breathed deeply, inhaling the lavender stuffed into the striking beak of his mask. Contentment washed over him as he pulled on thick gloves and took his staff to assume his place beside the woman. Hicks stood next to him, practically jittering with excitement.

Bayley spoke first, intoning the ancient prayer of a dead people, in a tongue long since vanished. His words carried power absolute, their syllables heavy with importance, weighted with ancient meaning. The air turned suddenly hot. A newfound strength emboldened Hereford and, he knew, the others.

The prostitute began to moan as consciousness slowly seeped into her. Her head turned from one shoulder to the other, eyes fluttering weakly. As her head moved,

Hereford caught sight of the frozen blood matting the hair behind her ear, where the resurrectionists had clubbed her into unconsciousness. Her limp hands shifted, and her panic clearly rose as she realized she could not raise her arms. Eyelids snapped open, and her mouth sounded an urgent but silent alarm, her scream lodged firmly in her throat. She attempted to kick her legs, but that effort, too, was useless. She was strapped tightly to the table. Bayley jammed a bite block into her mouth before buckling the leather straps at the back of her skull. Her scream growing thickly audible behind the wooden gag, she struggled all the more fervently, eyes wide with hysterical fright at the figures before her, until she began to choke. The six plague doctors lowered the razored appendages at the heads of their staffs, slicing away the whore's modest garments until she lay fully revealed.

Hereford's breath hitched in his throat, his heart racing at the sight of the woman's ample breasts, freed of their support and slumping to either side of her chest. Tears ran down her face. He followed the plane of her belly to the thick mat of dark-brown curls between her thighs. As his eyes roamed her, he noted the many slices to her skin left by the plague staffs. Each gash wept freely. She had clamped shut her eyes, unable to dam the tears pouring readily down her cheeks.

Suffering was the key, Bayley had said many months ago. And this woman's suffering was as sure as it was beautiful. She had to be aware of what came next, keenly focused on her pain and tormented by the understanding that her body was no longer her own. She was little more than a plaything, owned now by the beaked doctors gathered around her to do with her as they wished.

Bayley examined her eyes then spoke in that harsh, guttural dead tongue. The words were tinged with anger, as if the mere phonetics were built entirely from hate. The odd language roused the whore, drawing her attention to Bayley. The words had power, dangerous and dreadful power, and they triggered something instinctual and primitive within the woman. Frenzied, she attempted to rise despite the restraints pinning her cranium to the table. Her arms and legs struggled against the thick leather cuffs. Beads of sweat exploded along her hairline to run down her face, mingling with the current of tears blazing down her empurpled cheeks.

Light from the surrounding lanterns danced along the back of Hereford's razor. He stepped closer, holding the blade over the harlot's eyes, which widened in fear. He drew the flat of the blade across her collarbone then down her sternum. Her flesh turned bumpy, the fine hairs along her breasts standing on end. He dragged the flat edge across the rise of one breast, circling the areola. Her dark, ruddy nipple stiffened at the cool contact, and Hereford felt his own arousal growing. With his free hand, he pinched her nipple between thumb and forefinger, pulling it and stretching the elasticity of the breast to its peak. He slashed at her breast, a lightning quick strike to slice off the hardened pink nub in a sudden flair of violent theatrics. She screamed around the bite block, her cuffed hands slapping uselessly at the operating table. Tears and sweat washed down her pained, blanched-white face. A thick scarlet wash flooded across the pale mound of her ruined breast. Beneath his mask, Hereford licked his lips with longing.

Garbled pleading came from around the bite block, indecipherable and pointless. Her begging reached a crescendo as he amputated the other nipple, her head rising and slamming against the table repeatedly. Her breathing came in ragged gasps through her nose, reminding Hereford of wind rustling dead leaves and barren branches.

All the while, as he cut and goaded loose her screams, the plague doctors chanted their ancient hymn. Electric notes thickened the air as an unnatural heat rose to meet the last gasp of February cold. From the corner of his eye and through the darkened lens, Hereford saw a ripple in the air. He had seen similar apparitions before and knew that if he dared to look at it directly, it would disappear. The only way to see it was indirectly, at an angle, and through tinted glass.

The thinnie caught the woman's attention as well, and when she attempted to meet it head on, her pained expression took on a confused state. She had witnessed the impossible and knew not what to do with the information. Her pain briefly forgotten, she looked toward the beaked doctors with incredulity.

It was time to remind her, then. Hereford walked along the table's edge slowly, dragging the blade down her body as he went. One long, shallow, unbroken line split apart the skin of her flank. The razor bumped along the bony protrusions of her ribs then bit into her belly, cutting down the length of her and glancing across the curve of a hip bone. It continued down her shapely thigh and over her knee, to her shin and the top of her foot.

At the opposite end of the table, Bayley continued to read from his grimoire, while Post, Hicks, Ellery, and the sixth plague doctor, physician Douglas Quick, disassembled the woman's upper extremities. Hereford glanced up from his work to see Post gripping a mutilated breast in one hand, carving away at the fatty tissue with the other.

The woman's pain was incomparable, the bite block deadened her screams. She sought to thrash her head from side to side, but such movement was impossible. He had no doubt that if she were able, she would have slammed her skull against the table until she blacked out or caved her head in, in an attempt to escape the unyielding torment inflicted upon her.

The wet noise of tearing meat was very nearly drowned by the woman's muffled screams. Metal struck metal, then with the crack of bone, Ellery forced apart the whore's sternum. Meat tore free, and the woman turned silent, finally succumbing to death. Her eyes slammed shut, and a final shuddering breath shook her chest.

Ellery removed the heart and held it overhead, as if presenting an idol, then ceremoniously presented it to Hicks. He carried the heart to the nearby table and arranged it in its new cage, stabbing the wires into the appropriate spots along the ventricles and atria. He squeezed a sponge full of salty brine over the organ. In discordant rhythm, the trio of hearts began to beat in accordance to the voltaic charge. The crackle of electricity and the palpitations of flexing, strumming muscles danced in the air.

It's working, Hereford thought.

In his peripheral vision, his mouth slack with wonder, Hereford watched through the lenses of the plague mask as more thinnies opened in the air around him. Small slits split the air with a peculiar, silvery shine, then widened. As they grew, he saw the darkest of voids, an opening to an *elsewhere* that the candlelight could not reach. Bayley's voice thundered as he read from *Al Azif*, then Hereford saw movement deep within the holes, just hidden in the pitch blackness of the beyond, slithering in awareness.

No sooner did that thought occur to Hereford than the first heart lost its rhythm and slowed. The others followed, one by one, as the electric currents burned away the brine that propelled them. The thinnies closed.

Bayley tore loose his mask, a look of dejection painted across his features. All that remained in the operating theater were the remains of their awful, carnal depravity and the pungent reek of violent death.

Bayley's jowls trembled as he looked around the theater, his eyes finally settling on the slaughter at the room's center. "Clean this up," he said, waving at the messy disaster before him. "And dispose of… all of this."

Chapter 5

Salem Hawley kept watch over his friend's grave for three days. Each night, much like the body interned several feet below, grew colder and colder. Hawley, meanwhile, grew only more desperate and angry.

After their encounter with the body snatchers, Salem had hoisted Jeremiah over his shoulder, returned home with the man, and called for a local Negro physician to tend to him. Jeremiah's face had been shattered, his skull fractured in half a dozen places, and his teeth had been knocked out. He had been breathing, though— shallowly, at least. By the second day, his breathing had grown erratic, and a wet rattle clanged around inside his chest. Occasionally, he would cough, exhaling a red mist into the air above his lips. He slept and slept and would not wake.

Salem had been luckier, as his own injuries paled in comparison to Jeremiah's. His sides were a mess of bruises, the muscles of his back strained. Every breath he took renewed the deep ache in his tight chest, although, blessedly, no ribs had been fractured or broken. He hobbled around his small apartment like an old man, hunched over in pain. The worst injury, though, had been to his pride. Salem had taken far worse beatings from his former owner and the slave drivers the man employed, and he had the scars to prove it. His body would heal, he knew, but it was another thing altogether to recover from the mental recriminations that plagued him. Sitting beside Jeremiah, waiting and hoping for the man to awaken and rise, he was left only with his thoughts. If only he'd moved faster… If only Jeremiah hadn't been so brash, so impulsive in his anger…

Salem kept to the man's bedside until the last, shallow breath rattled Jeremiah's chest. After Jeremiah was laid to rest in the Negro cemetery, Salem remained with him, adamant that his friend's eternal rest would not be disturbed by those repugnant bands of roving grave robbers.

The cold nights did his injured body little good, and he would wake in the morning, freezing and stiff. To keep warm, he lined his clothes with old newspapers as well as more recent editions of the *Daily Advertiser*. Insulating him from the cold was a far nobler purpose for Childs's newspaper, which had taken to printing insults toward him of late.

He had sat beside Jeremiah's deathbed when the response to his Humanio letter caught his attention. The words of the entitled, self-important snob stuck both in his mind and his craw even days after the fact.

> *Great offence, it seems, has been given to some very tender and well-meaning souls by gentlemen of the medical department, for taking out of the common burying ground of this city bodies that had been interred there; one in particular, whose philanthropy is truly laudable, has obtained a place for his moving lamentations in your useful paper. Whence is skill in surgery to be derived? Kind and generous Humanio, your head is too empty, and your heart too full!*

That page of the *Advertiser* very nearly dripped condescension and derision, so soaked was it in malice. The author had signed off as "Junior, Broad Way" but gave no other means of identification. Hawley gave due consideration to tracking the man down, but such an effort would only incite further provocation and cause more grief.

With his left side resting against cold earth, Hawley wondered what the point of the war had been. For too long, the Negroes had been waiting for men to grant them the accords God had given freely. He spat, knowing all too well how God's words were twisted by the White devils. They believed the color of their skin granted them special privilege over others and that the darker one's skin was, the fewer human qualities they possessed. Negroes in particular were considered a subhuman species, and the attacks committed upon their bodies were nary seen as crimes at all. Hawley had lived in New York, right here in Manhattan, all his life. He'd fought, bled, and very nearly died for this country, the only nation he had ever known. Yet the idea of him even being equal was laughable. These Godly men did not even believe he, Jeremiah, or anyone of their ilk was as human as a Hessian who made himself a neighbor among the families he had been paid to slaughter.

Hawley had fought for his freedom, only to find his choices of where he could live and the jobs he could practice were limited. Even the sanctity of his burial was in doubt.

The Common Council did nothing with their complaints. If the bodies left to rot in the earth of the Negro cemetery and the potter's fields were to be left in peace, it fell upon the families to guard them and friends to offer safekeeping.

Perhaps that was the real lesson of the war, Hawley thought. One cannot wait to be given the freedoms God has guaranteed. One must take them. Seize them. And if they were denied, he must fight, and maybe kill, to claim them.

In that moment, Hawley realized two things with measured clarity. First, his war had perhaps not ended after all, and second, although he felt defeated, he was not finished fighting. And on the heels of that realization was a third revelation, an understanding that the Whites would not help stop the robberies of the Black graves until it began to impact them. They, too, would have to understand the personal sort of affront that particular brand of violation brought with it.

A plan began to take root.

He kissed the tips of his fingers and pressed them into the dirt as he said goodbye to his friend.

John Hicks, Jr. left his home on Broadway shortly past midnight to join up with his small band of grave diggers. Each teenager carried a wooden shovel over his shoulder. The moon was bright and the sky clear, making lanterns unnecessary. The stars provided more than enough light as the band of boys made their way toward Gold Street.

Passing a pig rummaging through the muck, Hicks reared back with his shovel and struck the animal along the spine at its hindquarters. The swine let out an angry scream as it ran away, Hicks's laughter chasing after it in the darkness. He had been in a foul mood the last few days, still reeling from the failed séance at the hospital, but striking the filthy beast had certainly felt good. His spirits were buoyed briefly, so much so that he looked forward to hitting something else.

Approaching the house of Scipio Gray, he thought he knew just what his target should be. He bounded up the steps of the Negro's porch and pounded on the man's front door.

"What are you doing?" one of his diggers whispered urgently.

Hicks smiled at the note of panic in the lad's voice and redoubled his efforts against the door.

"I'm coming," a baritone voice shouted from within the home. A moment later, the door opened.

As Gray opened his mouth to speak, Hicks punched him squarely in those fat Negro lips. Gray stumbled back, both hands going to his mouth, and Hicks shoved his way through the door, forcing the older man farther back.

"Get out of my house," Gray said, iron in his timbre.

The trio of diggers came in behind Hicks, and Scipio Gray darted his eyes from one to the next.

"Get to work," Hicks ordered them. Their footsteps clattered down the wooden porch as they retreated outside and filed into the field adjoining Gray's property.

With the Common Council refusing to act, Negroes who could afford it had taken to using Gray's private burial yard. Gray was custodian over the number of bodies buried there, and until that evening, those bodies had remained safe—far safer, at least, than those interred to the potter's field and the Negroes Burial Grounds.

Scipio took a step toward Hicks, intent on stopping him. Hicks was swifter, though, and he brought the shovel around, jabbing the wooden blade into the black man's belly. An electric thrill ran through the youth, and when Gray doubled over, Hicks launched himself forward, tackling the old man to the ground. Sitting astride Gray's chest, Hicks coiled his small fists and beat the man upon the face.

"I'm going to pop those fat nigger lips of yours like leeches," Hicks said. Beneath his knuckles, he felt teeth loosen and then a flood of hot, sticky warmth as skin burst.

Winded, Hicks pulled himself away and recovered his shovel. He thought about the nigger whose skull he had busted apart a short time ago, recalling how satisfying that was. Perhaps he was due an encore. He felt invigorated, strong, his whole body singing with energy. Beating a nigger was far more satisfying than smacking a swine on its rump. Of that much, he was certain.

He raised the shovel then brought the flat of its blade back down on Gray's belly. Air shot out of the man's lungs in a hearty gust, his pained moans filling the quiet home.

"Now, I got me some work to do," Hicks said. "You stay in here—you hear me? You as much as step one foot outside that door, I'll fucking kill you and burn your fucking house down."

Gray was in too much pain to respond. He merely nodded and waved his hand at Hicks, understanding lurking beneath the standing pool of water glistening in his eyes.

Hicks spat on the ground then turned on his heel.

Outside, his friends had already made progress unearthing a recent burial. Hicks joined the third boy, who was digging on his own, and began scooping away loose soil. He was grateful for the wooden shovels, which made less noise than their metal-bladed counterparts when striking rock, and these burial plots were certainly a rocky pair. After nearly an hour of digging, wood hit wood, and Hicks's shovel-mate dropped into the hole to break apart the head of the coffin. A similar scene played out behind him, as the other pair set about freeing the body within that plot.

"Ah, Jay-sus," the Irish boy said. Despite the cool air, he was sweating, and he swiped at his rosy dirt-streaked cheek with the sleeve of his coat.

"What?" Hicks said, crouching beside him.

"It's nothing but a wee baby. Lookit."

Hicks smiled, a wave of malice riding in him. "Too fucking perfect, then. Get it."

"It's nothing but a baby, John," Irish said, his words hardened with disgust.

"You bring out that fucking thing, or I bury you with it," Hicks said.

Irish shook his head, his eyes downcast. Nonetheless, he reached down and removed the mortal remains of a small infant, still wrapped in a swaddling blanket.

"What have you got?" Hicks asked, looking toward the other boys over his shoulder.

"Somebody's ol' grandmama."

"Just a shriveled old cunt," the other digger said. "Sure you want it?"

"Aye," Hicks said. "Get her out."

The boy in the hole hefted up the stiff remains of a weathered old soul. His partner in crime grabbed hold of her collar to help lift, then he got his arms under hers and pulled while the other shoved from below. Her heels drew lines in the dirt as she was pulled away from her resting place.

"It's your turn to carry," one boy demanded of the other. "I got the last one."

"Yeah, fine," the other digger said, hauling himself out of the hole. "Give her here then," he said, shouldering the load.

The boys headed toward the street. Irish held the small bundle in his arms, as if the child were still animate. His eyes were haunted, and Hicks clapped him on the back, grinning.

"A dead little nigger baby and a wizened old crone. This wasn't a bad haul," he said. Passing the front entrance of Gray's house, he caught sight of the old man standing in the doorway, watching them.

The free Black wiped at the blood on his lips with the back of a hand. "Aren't you ashamed of yourselves?" Gray shouted at their backs.

Hicks stopped, a cloud of expiration curling from his nostrils and drifting into the cold. "I'd do the same to my own granny," he said, smirking. "Cutting up that old bitch wouldn't hardly even be a crime!"

Laughing, he skipped away, chasing after his diggers. He was in too good of a mood to argue, even with a spent old nigger.

Word spread fast through the community of the bodies snatched away from Scipio Gray's private yard and of the violent youths who had stormed his property and threatened to kill him. By the time Hawley heard of the attack, he and Prince were just finishing the boy's lessons for the day and were ready to break for lunch prior to his afternoon chores. Hawley gave Prince an almost-paternal pat on the head as he said his goodbyes, then he gathered his few belongings and left, resolved to visit Scipio.

Although Scipio's was out of the way, Hawley felt an urgent pull toward the man's property, and his feet carried him along rather swiftly. When the man finally answered his door upon Hawley's insistent knocking, Hawley let loose a gasp of surprise. Scipio's face was uneven and lumpy with a number of swollen knobs. Each shined with a bruise. The man's lips were puffy and braided with thick scabs. Beyond the lips were several empty spaces where teeth should have been.

"My God," Hawley said.

Scipio couldn't meet the younger man's eyes. Staring at the floor, Scipio nodded slightly and made way for Salem's entrance.

His fingers curled tightly around the brim of his hat, Hawley asked, "How bad are you hurt?"

Scipio shrugged then winced. He led his visitor to a pair of chairs and slowly lowered himself into a seat.

"I'll endure. It is my pride that has been more gravely wounded, I fear. Children, Salem—children did this to me."

This time, it was Hawley who shrugged. "I've met my share of vicious children, friend. They can be surprising, particularly if underestimated."

"They took me by surprise. I thought a late bit of business came to my door, but I was not expecting to meet a fist when I opened it."

"They threatened you, I heard."

"One boy did." Scipio raised his head, less shy now that he was settled in his favorite seat. "The ringleader of those little vandals. The other three, he put to work."

"Can you describe him?"

"He's on the smaller side, which I suppose makes it so he has quite a lot more to prove to most boys. He's stronger than he looks, with a vicious streak no boy his age should possess." Scipio provided what details he could on the boy's physical appearance, but his recollection was murky, having observed his attacker largely through a fog of tears and pain.

Hawley nodded, weighing the information. "I believe these bandits are the same as killed Jeremiah and stole the remains of his beloved and their precious child."

Scipio's jaw fell, his tongue sliding briefly between his lips before being sucked back inside. "They're dangerous, Salem. The boy in particular. He is pure evil, I fear."

"They cannot be allowed to continue as they've been," Hawley said. "An end must be brought to them for our people to have any peace of mind."

A hint of a smile played out upon Scipio's face, a gleam in his eyes. "And it's you to bring such an end to them, eh?" When he chuckled, it came forth with a liquid, gravelly rumble.

"The council refuses to act. The night watchmen

refuse to act. Somebody must do something."

Scipio regarded his friend, a stern glint in his eyes. "You best mind yourself, then. I won't see your bastard husk resurrected."

Hawley laughed, the first laugh in days; it warmed him. Scipio joined him, clutching his belly in obvious pain but unable to quit his humor.

"Ah, hell, that hurts," he complained, which only made Hawley laugh harder. After a time, their enjoyment waned, and a somber tone resettled upon them. "Is there anything you need from me?"

After a moment's consideration, Hawley said, "No. Not yet."

"That boy is due his comeuppance," Scipio said. He seemed on the verge of saying more, his eyes glistening. Hawley waited for him to continue, and finally he did. "That child's cruelty, the evil in his eyes... Maybe I'm crazy, but it's as if, in those moments, he had put me back into those old chains. I forgot my place in those moments, you understand?"

Hawley nodded. He reached across to the armrest and curled his fingers around Scipio's hand, giving him a gentle squeeze. He felt his own tears rising then, weighted with a measure of guilt. His friends and community were being terrorized, and he could no longer stand idle while it continued. He had delayed much too long already.

He rose, clutching his hat once more, a fresh hatred settling in his heart. He knew what he must do. "I promise, if I need anything at all, you'll be the first I'll call upon."

He gave Scipio a quick but firm embrace and let himself out. It took his eyes a moment to adjust to the brightness of day after having spent such a time in the dark.

Hawley's feet crunched through a frozen shell of snow as he plodded over the uneven ground of the Trinity churchyard. Even under the golden glow of moonlight reflecting brilliantly off the icy white surface, he found it hard going. He had nearly twisted his ankle walking over a hillock of freshly turned soil buried beneath the snow, a fresh grave he surmised, and perhaps a sprained ankle served him right, given his injurious plans for this evening. This grave, he decided, was as good as any other.

With his back to the picket fence outlining the churchyard, he cast a look at the darkened and empty church before him. He thought of offering a prayer but knew his soul was beyond saving. What the priests said of forgiveness mattered little in the end, and even if God were to forgive him for this particular trespass, he was not sure he could ever forgive himself.

A vaporous cloud bloomed off his lips as he let out a weary sigh, then he put his back to it. The wooden shovel blade bit into snow, cracking the fragile, frozen shell, then struck the stiff resistance of cold earth. Hawley stepped upon the shoulder of the blade, his weight forcing the shovel deeper, and scooped away clods of dirt. In no time at all, his back grew stiff and achy, and his heart pounded hard with the exertion. Sweat bloomed beneath his cap, along his forehead, and his hands turned hot beneath his gloves. He checked his surroundings periodically, afraid he would be spotted. It was a bastard of a job this digging, but after an hour, he hit the lid of the coffin interned there in the burial plot.

His heart raced, but no longer solely from the exertion of this chore. He took yet another look around the churchyard before lowering himself into the hole, certain that he was still undiscovered. The wooden boards of the coffin creaked beneath his feet. He jimmied the shovel blade into the dirt-caulked crack between the lid's boards and pulled the handle back. The top half of the first board broke free, and he moved onto the next.

The woman inside was youthful, her hair golden under the moonlight. Her white face was softly rounded, her nose upturned at the tip. Had she been alive, Hawley might have admired her cute features, and he wondered, briefly, if she had carried a certain charm about her in her previously animated state. Shamefully, he banished those thoughts. The chore held no charming appeal for him, and he could not linger. Already, he felt as if his time were running out, and he worried he would be discovered at any moment.

He flung the shovel over the lip of the grave then bent down to retrieve the woman. As he hauled her free of her resting place, she was loose limbed. The rigor mortis that would have seized her muscles had already passed. The smell of death, however, lingered, and he turned his face away from the body, gasping for the fresh, cold bite of winter air. Each inhalation, unfortunately, was stained with musky, fecund rot that was inescapable even as he breathed through his mouth.

The resurrectionists, he knew, stripped the cadavers before absconding with the bodies. The reason was simple—though grave robbing was illegal, body snatching, however morally dubious and perverse, was not. Given that such thefts had been limited to the Negro graves or the remains of the poor populating the potter's field, the Common Council had not seen fit to invent new laws to act as a deterrence.

Perhaps now that shall change, Hawley thought. He dropped the woman's body to the cold earth and drew his blade. He pressed the knife's edge against a taut piece of dress, but his hand was indecisive. He could not bring himself to cut loose her garments. He tried again, the guilt weighing down upon him.

"Damn it," he said, so softly the words were barely audible to his own ears. He returned the knife to his pocket then hoisted the woman, still clothed and bejeweled, over his shoulder.

Plotting his steps carefully, he retraced his path back to the fence and out of the churchyard, listening for the voices of watchmen or, worse, the shipyard ruffians and drunken rowdies who freely caroused the city streets, searching for violence and hungry for blood. He kept to the shadows and hoped the pale countenance of his cargo was not white enough to draw attention his way. He mentally cursed himself, already regretting his actions and knowing the worst was yet to come.

If he couldn't even remove her clothes, Hawley wasn't sure how he would manage what lay ahead. *You stupid fool!*

He could not take the body back to his apartment, for various reasons, least of which was the smell. Such an effort was risky and required covering too much ground. He had to secret the body away somewhere that was both safe and nearby, where he could work for several hours without being discovered.

Hawley's head sank under the weight of his thoughts, his stomach roiling. Bitter heat rose up his middle, a savage cramp twisting his belly, as a singular realization hit home—he could not do what he'd come to do.

His knees buckled, and the corpse slid off his

shoulders and out of his arms. The body hit muddy earth with a wet slap, and in reflex, Hawley's hands darted out to break his fall. His knees sank into wet, freezing earth; black snow squeezed between his fingers. Bile kicked loose from his stomach, burning its way up and ejecting in a searing spray. For several long moments, he stayed on hands and knees, dry heaving over the puddle of his own waste.

The woman in white lay on her back, her head lolled toward him. Her open eyes, though vacant, had somehow found his. His gut lurched, and it felt like his innards were sloshing against his spine, attempting to force their way out of him on another tide of vomit. A thick line of drool dangled from his lip, slinking toward the slush he knelt in.

Digging her up, disturbing her rest, and stealing her corpse—all of that had been quite bad enough, quite literally making him sick. He knew he could proceed no further with his plan.

The resurrectionists would dissect her if given the chance. Her organs would be pulled from their cavities, her limbs torn from her trunk piece by piece, her body dismembered and then cut into pieces to be dumped up and down the streets and shores of Manhattan. That was what those body-snatching trash would do. Salem Hawley was not among their number, though. He could never do that, not ever. Not without losing whatever was left of his soul.

The wooden handle of his hatchet was heavy against his thigh, and he knew too well the evil purpose he had intended for it this eve. He could couch his actions up to this point in some perverted form of nobility. He could consider this a small bit of evil to do a larger work of good for his people. He could justify all this as recompense for the memories of friends lost, for those who have suffered at the depraved hands of grave robbers and body snatchers. But he could not lie to himself.

Snow fell gently, to melt against the exposed stretches of his black flesh. The white flakes slowly accumulated atop the dead woman's body, whiter than she was pale. He decided to leave her here, then, in the alley. Perhaps the snow, for a time, would bury her. Mayhap she might even find the rest he had denied her, if for but a day, or a handful of days.

He rose slowly, his joints aching in the cold, his body numb despite the burning heat of shame that trembled his limbs. The woman's eyes followed him as he rose. He met her gaze for a final time and directed a nod toward her before quickly discarding the inchoate prayer on his lips. He could offer her no words of prayer. Nor did he expect forgiveness from her or anything else that lay beyond the realm of life itself. Certainly his soul was damned, and this night had done little to ease that burden. He shook as fingers of cold danced across his neck, chiding himself for his self-pity. He had done wrong, and it was not for his soul he must grieve, but for the woman, whose name he did not even know.

He nodded again, this time more to himself, and turned on his heels. He shuffled through the accumulating snow, a caul of cold air wrapping him in its violent embrace. The handle of his hatchet danced against his thigh with every step, the promise of violence coiling within him with every tap and shush of the wood against his pants and the long overcoat that covered it. His night of devilry was over. *But only for this night*, he thought. It was only the first eve of necessary evil. More were on the way, as sure as the snow and ice.

100 Dollars REWARD

*Whereas one night last week, the grave
of a person recently interred in Trinity
Churchyard was opened, and the
Corpse, with part of the clothes, were
carried off.*

*Any person who will discover the
offenders, so that they may be convicted
and brought to justice, will receive the
above reward from the Corporation of
the Trinity Church.*

> *By Order of the Vestry
> Robert C. Livingston, Treasurer
> New York Feb. 21, 1788*

From The Daily Advertiser

*We have been in a state of great
tumult for a day or two past. The causes
of which, as well as I can digest from
various accounts, are as follows: The
young students of physic have, for some
time past, been loudly complained of for
their very frequent and wanton trespasses
in the burial grounds of this City. The
corpse of a young gentleman from the
West Indies was lately taken up, the
grave left open and the funeral clothing
scattered about. A very handsome and
much-esteemed young lady of good
connection was also carried off. These,
with various other acts of a similar
kind, inflamed the minds of people
exceedingly, and the young member of
the faculty as well as the mansions of the
dead, have been quickly watched.*

Chapter 6

Knots exploded in a series of loud pops as the fire chewed through the wooden logs. The first sizzling bang startled Hereford, nearly making him leap free of his skin. For a brief moment, he was on the battlefield once more, decade-old memories rushing to the forefront of his mind with the sound of gunfire and the screaming of injured men, some of them little more than children. He smelled not the pleasant odor of burning pine but of burning flesh and gunpowder.

As the fire consumed the wood, a trio of rapid explosions boomed through Dr. Bayley's study. Finally,

Hereford calmed, recognizing the noise for what it was. Still, it took a long moment for his heart's pace to steady and even.

Bayley, who had been speaking and noticed Hereford's surprised reaction, gave him a queer look, eyeing him over the rim of his brandy glass.

"Is something troubling you?" Bayley asked.

"The sudden noise shook me is all."

Hereford felt like a child under Bayley's gaze, and he could feel the older man sizing him up, judging his worth. In some ways, many of them minor, Bayley remind Hereford of his own father. Although the doctor was prone to fewer fits of violence, and when he was in his cups, Bayley was certainly much more delightful than Hereford's father had ever been. Bayley shrugged, and whatever Hereford had glimpsed in the man's eyes disappeared, as if washed away with the sip of brandy.

"Ah." Bayley stood and prodded the logs in the fireplace with a long tool, stoking the flames. They seized upon the fresh logs quickly, with a throaty growl. Satisfied, Bayley returned to his amply padded leather wingback chair, crossed his legs at the knee, and resumed his idle sipping. "Now then. Where were we?"

"The impetuousness of young Mr. Hicks," Hereford supplied.

"Ah, yes. So, do you believe him?"

"He claims, rather adamantly, to know nothing of the Trinity Church theft. I've pressed him on this issue several times, but the story he retreats to is the same. He is, I suspect, telling the truth."

Bayley used his thigh as a platform to spill some tobacco on a rolling paper then set about lighting it. He seemed to savor the long inhalation, holding the smoke in his lungs for a long moment, then he exhaled with an exaggerated care, uneager to release the thick cloud from his lips.

"It's makes no matter, I suppose. Issues of his involvement aside, I suspect the resentment and unease this theft has caused will suit our needs nicely." Bayley smiled then, the slight crease of his lips tight and chilly.

Hereford tilted his head in agreement then took a sip of hot tea to soothe the soreness lingering in his throat. He had spent much of the morning coughing, but the cold he was afflicted with seemed to ease in the evening hours, its brutality an effect of the morning.

"I understand it caused quite the ruckus at the Common Council," Hereford said, recalling the *Daily Advertiser's* story of heated words and rising tempers between the assemblymen and the illiterates whose interests they supposedly represented. He himself had been more than a bit chuffed to see his advertisement offering anatomy lessons placed alongside a rebuttal to an earlier opine by Humanio from a one "Junior, of Broad Way," whom he took to be the sanctimonious man-child John Hicks, Jr.

"I have no doubt," Bayley said. "But this could be the key component that our earlier experimentations have failed to capitalize upon. Think of it, Jonathan."

Leaning forward in his chair, one elbow propped on his knee to keep the rolled tobacco raised at the ready, Bayley continued. "We have been attempting to draw forth these otherworldly elementals with a rich cocktail of blood and fear and even more than a bit of theatrics."

Hereford knew he meant the rig of hearts and voltaic piles. But even those minor contraptions had been speculation born of Abd al-Hazred, whose *Al Azif* spoke of uncaged hearts still beating succulent promises to be savored by the Ancients. The text, however, was unclear on how philosophical, figural, or literal the passage was to be understood. The accompanying spate of Greek,

Latin, French, Chinese, German, Arabic, and English translations of the Sumerian original shed little light and, in some instances, only added to the confusion. As the *Al Azif* was translated and retranslated from one language to the next, inconsistencies had crept in. Several key words had been misinterpreted or replaced with imperfect substitutions. Others, though, had clearly attempted to decipher Abd al-Hazred's ancient puzzle with modern technology, leaving notes dating back to the Sasanian Empire from the time of 224 AD. The inventor described the creation of a battery using terracotta pots, a cylinder of rolled copper sheeting, an iron rod, and an acidic liquid to generate an electric current. This battery was quite similar to the Leyden jar. Its inventor, a cleric named Ewald Georg von Kleist, had also made notes of his experiments circa 1740 in pages folded into *Al Azif.* As Benjamin Franklin had previously confirmed, von Kleist noted that linking multiple batteries together produced a stronger charge. Over the years, Bayley had become quite the student of electricity, following the work of Luigi Galvani and Alessandro Volta, who originated designs for the voltaic piles that Bayley had constructed.

"Our scope has been lacking," Bayley said. "We have been far too narrow in our methodology."

The thought had occurred to Hereford, but he had not spoken of it to the other plague doctors. Perhaps, upon reflection, he should have spoken of it at least to his mentor, Bayley.

"Those beings we witnessed were drawn by the allure of mass casualties," Hereford said.

Bayley's eyes widened in excitement. "Yes! Exactly! Exactly that! What is the fear of but one simple nigger, street urchin, or whore compared to scores ten deep of the wounded and dying, of those whose life is bleeding out from between their very fingers as they stand on the precipice of death's door?"

Caught up in his whirlwind, Bayley clapped his hands together then screwed the rolled tobacco between his lips, taking to his feet. He puffed away happily, striding back and forth across his study.

"We constrained ourselves in the name of science, of experimentation. And now we have discovered but one mode of practice to be an ill fit toward achieving our goals. Our methodology has been necessarily limited through a systematic process of elimination. We allowed ourselves to be blinded by the vestiges of our welfare, of our own need for secrecy and safety. I believe this was not in error, however, but a simple process to allow for our minds to become both broadened and emboldened. We see now what must be done, and we have practiced accordingly while the stars aligned themselves. Do you agree?"

Hereford had never seen his mentor in such a state of wild, exuberant agitation, and he felt a gust of bravado sweep through him as he was caught up in the moment. "Yes, I do! I do believe this is our time."

On the battlefield, he had witnessed no shortage of horrors, seen no bottom to the depths of mankind's depravities. But he had also seen something remarkable, something magnificent and beautiful. Something pure and lovely to counterbalance the plague of humanity. It had approached total awe in its maleficence as, one by one, it sucked away the life of those wounded, dying soldiers. Humanity was little more than sets of warring tribes, trading in rape and murder and slavery, fighting tooth and nail to scrabble out whatever small purchase it could win, and all the while praising God as if he were something other than a righteous joke. Hereford had seen real gods during the war and since that day, he had lived for them. He had killed for them, and if necessary, he would die for them.

The whores he had taken knives and scalpels and axe blades to had been but a meager prelude. The bodies stolen from graveyards were little more than a means to an end, and he saw now the end goal it had all been leading toward. Merely spilling blood was not enough. It must be on a grand scale.

Manhattan was an island of fear. Even the Whites now slept atop their loved ones' graves to protect the deceased from the brutish resurrectionists, and rowdies roamed the streets, looking for any reason to fight, hoping to take matters of justice into their own drunken hands. Promises of rewards were routinely published in the city's various newspapers or loudly barked about by urchins in the street. Pockets of violence breaking out within cemetery grounds overnight were no longer uncommon. Doctors and anatomists like Hereford and Bayley were hated for their callous looting and ribald destruction of corpses. Speaking in hushed whispers and with elbows touching, tavern-goers gossiped, and each word passing their emboldened lips held a hint of antagonism, and more to the point, terror and suspicion.

The city was at a tipping point. All that was needed was one solid shove. Then the plague doctors would have their fear and bloodshed, along with the promise of death on a necessarily grand scale, to lure forth their dark and ancient gods.

The specimen was laid bare before John Hicks, Jr. She was middle-aged, and her skin was porcelain white. A chill from the cold earth still emanated from her body even after she'd been stationed overnight in the third-floor dissection room. Her brown hair was tied into a bun and acted as a sort of pillow for her head. The stink of death was still fresh upon her, and he inhaled it greedily as he lowered his head to her bared sex and smiled. Certain that none of his classmates were watching, he quickly kissed her vulva, a thrill rushing through him at such a public display of affection.

His heart very nearly tore free of his chest when a shout cut through the gray skies, and he jerked upright, scalpel in hand. None of the other students were paying him the slightest attention, and after a moment of further shouts and youthful laughter, he determined the noise was coming from outside. Sure enough, despite the looming presence of black clouds and the promising threat of rain, a group of children were playing in the yard below. He recognized the youngest as Patrick O'Reilly, whose mother had recently passed after a protracted illness. She had sought the consult of Dr. Bayley not long before her expiration. Recovering her from her burial box had been surprisingly easy, given the fever of fear that had gripped so many Manhattanites of late.

A smile spread across Hicks's lips as he traded scalpel for saw and set to work on the corpse. Although the other students chatted amiably with one another, they rarely spoke to him unless something demanded it and gave him a wide berth in which to conduct his work. He ignored their useless babble, enraptured instead by the sound of metal teeth sawing through soft flesh then sturdy bone. The arm came free at the elbow, and he practically laughed, a fit of mania swelling up within him.

In three paces, he was back at the window, shoving it open. A cold gust blew in immediately, and the students shouted in surprise.

"Close that damn window!"

Holding the arm by elbow stump, he waved the hand outside the window. Affecting a parody of an Irish accent, he called out, "Oh, Patty-boy! Oh, Patty-boy, look what I've got here!"

The boy looked up toward the third-floor window, his eyes going large and round, mouth agape. His friends ceased their antics as well, all eyes on Hicks.

"I got your sweet old mum!" Hicks waved the arm back and forth in an exaggerated greeting, baring his teeth in a wolfish smile. "Come watch me fuck her dried-up cunny!"

"Close the window, you fuck!" another shout came.

Hicks could not contain his laughter any longer. He brought the pale, bloodless hand to his crotch, his hips making lewd thrusting motions toward the window. The children were shouting over one another, and he laughed all the harder as O'Reilly's friends pulled him away from the hospital. The ginger-haired boy was red-faced and furious, tears streaming down his face.

"I'll even let you have a turn!" Hicks shouted at their retreating backs, cackling madly.

Two of his fellow students gripped him by the arms and pulled him away. Once Hicks was clear, another student stepped into the gap and pulled shut the window, swearing all the while. Hicks continued laughing, a stitch in his ribs and out of breath. He used the dead woman's hand to wipe away the tears.

Donald O'Reilly listened to his son's story, apprehension mounting alongside a good deal of frustration as Patrick fought through his competing rage and sorrow. The boy's anger made him inarticulate, and it took a good deal of time to calm him enough to make sense.

In the days following Carolyn's passing, Donald had spent much of the time alone in his own grief. He made an effort to stay strong for Patrick, keeping his emotions in check and working to lay bricks every day to keep the boy well fed. As night fell, though, he sobbed quietly to himself, in a marriage bed occupied only by himself and a cold emptiness, until sleep claimed him. He felt himself on the brink, tiptoeing a dangerous edge. His temper was short and his tongue quicker than it had ever been in the past, and he found himself seeking escape in both loneliness and liquor. He had been happy for Patrick to take leave with his friends, allowing Donald the opportunity to cry in solitude. He'd spent much of the morning crying into his cups, killing his pain and his grief with harsh whiskey. Patrick's words sobered him up right quick and put a rod of hell-forged steel right in his spine.

First, he gathered his shovel. Then he pounded on the doors of men he knew he could trust, fellow masons he worked with regularly. They were hard, solid men who would have his back if the need arose.

As a group, the men, armed with shovels and picks, made their way to the cemetery. Confirmation was needed before all else. Donald took shovel to earth, the churned dirt coming away easily. After a short time, he and his friends revealed Carolyn's coffin. The head of the box had been broken away. The removed wood had dropped into the hole and was covered by dirt. Aside from earth and rock, the coffin was empty. Carolyn was gone.

His cheeks burned beneath the beginnings of a cold rain. "Now, lads, I aim to bring my wife back."

He looked at each man squarely, eye to eye, and each nodded his support.

"We're with you," their foreman said.

Although many of the men had not lost a family member in such similar fashion, they had at least heard accounts of the body snatching and gossiped about it aplenty as they worked. If not directly impacted themselves, most knew people whose grieving had been made all the worse by those night raiders. The space separating them from the victimized was made all the smaller that day.

"To the hospital then," Donald said. He led the small group from the cemetery grounds and down Broadway, drawing a crowd in their wake as they marched to the hospital on Pearl Street.

Hawley pushed into the warm, velvety folds of Abbie's sex as if he were thrusting through the gates of heaven. He gripped her breasts in both hands. Her feet hung in the air just above the shelf of his buttocks, below the network of scars crisscrossing the expanse of his back and hips. She knew better than to touch his back.

Sweaty and breathless, she encouraged him. "That's it, baby," she moaned. "That's it… that's it."

His face twisted in a spasm of pleasure as she squeezed the muscles of her canal, gripping him tightly as he pushed deeper.

She laughed pleasantly, her arms tossed overhead across the pillow her kinky hair was splayed upon, then whispered, "Oh yes."

His hands moved to her hips as he rose to his knees, his breathing growing more ragged and shallow. The sounds of his pleasure were lost beneath the noise of their skin smacking together until he let out a fierce cry and pulled free. Her hand immediately went to his member, enthusiastically stroking him over the rise of her belly as a wave of release jolted through him and left him shuddering in the wake of orgasm.

"Sweet Jesus," he said breathlessly.

She pumped him a few more times, the last of his seed pooling across her fingers and dripping to the puddle on her belly. Spent, he collapsed next to her, his hands folded across his stomach. She ran her fingers playfully through the damp curls of his chest hair.

"It's always so nice when you visit me, darling," she said.

He opened his mouth to speak, but a rowdy noise from the street below cut him off. Men were shouting, their words incoherent. He peeled away from Abbie and strode across the candlelit room, naked still and led by a wilting erection, to the window opposite. The thick drapes were so effective at blocking out the day, he had forgotten it was still early. Despite the overcast sky, his eyes took a moment to adjust to the brightness. A crowd was gathering outside the saloon, led by men carrying shovels, picks, and axes. Turning an ear toward them, he caught snatches of curses aimed at the city's doctors and word of violated graves. He snickered at the thought that, seemingly, the Whites would not tolerate being victimized. Perhaps Humanio's work was to be paid off at last. His robbery of Trinity Church had apparently emboldened the rogue resurrectionists to begin targeting White burial grounds with as much enthusiasm as they had previously reserved for the Blacks.

He peeked through the curtains for a moment, watching the angry mob pushing farther down Broadway. If they continued straight on down, they would reach New York Hospital in due time.

Abbie pushed up on her elbows, long curls of black hair spilling over her breasts. "What's happening?"

"Sounds like they're going after the doctors, maybe." He answered with a shrug then set about collecting his clothes off the floor.

"About time."

Earlier, downstairs, she had briefly shared rumors with him of other ladies in her profession who had gone missing. A few had turned up in the streets, mutilated and dismembered, dumped in alleyways with the trash.

"Some had organs missing," she had whispered, visibly shaken, telling him rumors of how students of the physic were, perhaps, no longer content with mauling only the dead.

Rumors had stacked up atop one another, trailing through town across a grapevine of speculation and distrust. Missing prostitutes was a thing rarely spoken of, and as far as he knew, the resurrectionists had yet to be implicated in such disappearances. He listened intently to her gossiping nevertheless.

A charge, something electric, pulsed through the air. Manhattan carried a peculiar rhythm on the best of days, but even that felt upset in the commotion. He had to get downstairs, for the sake of Jeremiah and Scipio, and all the things they had lost. He pulled free several bills, folded them, and pressed them into Abbie's slender hands. "Would you do me a favor?"

When she nodded, he asked her, "Round me up Scipio, tell him what's occurred and where I'm going. I need him to join me at New York Hospital as quickly as he can. Go now, but please, be careful."

She nodded again, searching for a towel to wipe away the deposit he had left upon her torso, while he dressed. Candlelight reflected off the sheen of sweat covering her, giving her skin a bronze glow. He took a moment to admire her then finished with his belt and boots. She dressed quickly then followed him downstairs, where they went in opposite directions.

Hers was the quiet path, away from trouble. Salem Hawley followed the noise of angry White men and clattering tools readied for war.

From inside the dissection room, it sounded as if the whole of New York Hospital was surrounded by a mad cacophony. Hicks gazed out upon the yard, and although the windows were shut firmly, the quarrelsome shouting and screamed demands reached his ears. It was all just so much noise, though, with the mob yelling over one another, their message reduced to a thunderously incoherent mess.

"What is all that?" one student asked, looking

up from the study of a male subject's internal organs. Curious, he set aside his instruments and wiped his hands as he approached Hicks.

"This is your doing," another said, directing his scorn squarely at Hicks.

Below, a single man stepped forward, shovel in hand. "I want all you doctors out here, right fucking now!" His booming voice had a gravelly edge to it, powerful and smoky.

Hicks turned to the students beside him and flashed them both a toothsome, winning smile. "I do believe these gathered gentlemen are requesting your presence in the yard." He laughed then put his back to the window and the boys. Ignoring the growing clamor, he took up his scalpel and carved fresh lines into the dead woman at his station. He cut simply to cut, with no rhyme or reason. He slashed at pearlescent skin for the sheer enjoyment of it, opening dry, parted lips in her belly, thighs, and forearms.

One student studied Hicks with unveiled disgust before his eyes turned back toward the window with worry. He ran his hands through his hair, plainly unsure whether he was better off inside with a crazed, young sadist or outside amid a throng bent on violence.

"We go out the back," another student said.

"They could have the whole building surrounded," one objected.

"Don't know till we try, boys," a third said.

"Yes, yes," Hicks chimed in. "Out the back, it is, then. Best move fleet of foot!" Again, his maniacal laughter bubbled up as his blade cut a long, solitary line down the woman's abdomen. "Out, out, out!"

The teenage anatomists shook their heads in disgust. Behind them, a rock crashed through the window, raining shards of glass upon the floor. The noise was enough to compel the students to flee, and they jostled one another as they vied to be the first out of the room.

Hicks trailed behind them, taking his time. He tapped a mindless rhythm against his pant leg with the flat edge of his scalpel, whistling softly to himself. Footfalls echoed through the stairwell as the boys thundered down the steps, encouraging one another to move faster. Shouting from the crowd outside seemed to dog their each and every step, and still, Hicks whistled, savoring the stink of adolescent fear leeching off the boys.

He hit the ground floor and turned toward the rear of the building. Panic and anger echoed along the hallway from opposite directions, but he followed the corridor to the operating theater, which was currently closed. The boys yanked at the doors on either side of the theater, their panic growing with the discovery that those doors were locked as well.

And then, with sudden swiftness, the theater doors were pulled open. Light from the hallway spilled into the darkened auditorium to reveal a gathering of black-clad, beak-faced bodies bearing scalpels. The boys startled. One let loose a scream. Then the plague doctors were upon them, seizing the moment of surprise. Blades sank into bellies and slashed at faces.

One boy turned, but Hicks was already standing there with a devilish grin spread upon his face. It was the last thing the boy would see, as Hicks raised his own scalpel and drew it across the younger child's throat. A plume of air whistled softly from the boy's severed windpipe, and a fountain of blood sprayed from either side of his neck. His hand rose but failed to stop the red gushing jet.

Hicks strode forward, slashing at the backs of the children before him, while his fellow cultists brutalized them from the front. Soon, the wooden floorboards were soaked with blood, and the plague doctors hauled the bodies inside the operating theater.

Not all of the boys were dead, however. Two still clung to life, if only by the edge of but one fingertip. Their breaths were shallow and clearly pained, and with each exhalation, they expelled pure, raw fear.

Hicks slammed shut the doors to the theater, muffling the madness outside. The crowd was growing violently loud, and it likely would not be long before they got their druthers up enough to force their way inside.

Bayley stood at the front of the theater, a large tome in hand, reading aloud. A pair of plague doctors pulled the boys into the center of the room and kicked at the backs of their knees, forcing them to the floor. They stood behind the boys, scalpels at the necks of both teens. Bayley's gloved fingers moved over thin onionskin pages. Between the periodic pauses of Bayley's chanting, the voltaic piles hummed, driving dead muscle given unsure life. The trio of hearts beat within their cages, and blue arcs of light flashed, delivering electric charge from the batteries to the briny solution that soaked the hearts. The chambers of each heart beat bloodlessly, out of rhythm with the electric crackle.

Hicks did not understand a single word Bayley spoke, but he could feel the power each syllable carried. The language, dark and ancient, drove into the air around them. The room, by turns, grew stifling hot and arctic cold, a wind fueled by the slurry of magic Bayley recited. Beneath the cloak he had donned, Hicks could feel the hairs all along his arms and the back of his neck stand on end. An invisible weight coiled around his middle. A tight, unseen muscle hugged him closely as hot breath pulsed against the side of his face. Something crawled across him, up his legs, and over his jaw. A breeze rustled his bare head as spiky-haired fingers pried open his mouth, then a hot, pulsating, multi-legged thing crawled past his lips and bit into his tongue.

He screamed, but his cries of pain were ignored. A thunderous crash assaulted his ears from both inside and outside the room. Hicks jerked and writhed in agony, seeking escape from whatever had grabbed hold of him. His fingers searched for the foreign body biting at the inside of his mouth but found nothing, nothing at all. He saw the air all around him ripple and spasm. The front doors had been breached, and the mob was coming for all of them.

Bayley read, his voice rising to an impossible tenor over the fury set upon the air, the skies, and the heavens. And then the air itself pulled apart, and the wind kicked up, nearly knocking Hicks off his feet. He saw stars—actual physical stars—set against a black void, hanging in the air before him. The air had peeled open to reveal a nightscape, but there were things between the stars, beasts his mind could not comprehend, creatures his eyes refused to see. They were there, nonetheless.

A flash of lightning lit up the room, then an eerie darkness crashed down upon them. Bayley turned another impossibly thin page, screaming now as he read. Long, muscular tendrils pierced the veil between worlds, hanging in the air before Hicks and the other doctors. Looking down, he saw, for the first time, the thick appendage gripping him, hoisting him off his feet. Tentacles seized both his arms, tearing his searching hands away from his face, just as fresh pain exploded in his mouth. He screamed, a well of blood rising from the cavity of his mouth, surging from between the gaps in his teeth, and he spat out his severed tongue. Rough, spidery limbs brushed against the inner walls of his cheeks, and still, he screamed as pointed mandibles stabbed into his upper palate, boring through the roof of his mouth. The tentacle squeezed, hard enough to pop something inside Hicks's middle, breaking a trio of ribs. The sharp end of bone pierced a lung, and the air went out of him on a cry of torment.

As he recoiled in pain, dizzy with the fever of fear, he saw his final moments. Bayley turned another page, and the plague doctors violently slashed at the throats of the kneeling boys. Bright-red arcs ejected in the wake of their blades, then their young forms slumped and toppled. Strangely, their blood did not similarly fall but was held suspended between their prone forms and the thinnie growing above them. The crimson bubbles danced in the air, weightless. The blossoming darkness above them shimmered and resolved, and inky, ephemeral limbs snaked through the void, searching for handholds upon the dead children and finding succor.

The strain of Hicks's agony grew so loud that tendons in his neck popped and his voice went hoarse. His torment teetered uncontrollably toward insanity. Driven to madness by the profound misery, his mind fractured into its final disassembled form as a jointed, fuzzy limb shot out through his nostril, scrabbling over his upper lip for purchase as it continued to eat its way upward through his skull. The creature burrowed into some cavity within his face. Pressure built behind his eyes then exploded outward.

His last sight was of a massive, slumbering beast awakening. The last he heard was of a banging of metal against wood, the mob demanding entry into the auditorium. The last he felt was the air being pulled from his one good lung, and he exhaled in obligation.

Chapter 7

An impossible wind staggered Hereford on his heels as his brain struggled to comprehend the images set before him. From the corner of his eyes, he saw shimmering thinnies dancing all through the auditorium, and through those thinnies came the searching tendrils of the inexplicable. Puckered tentacles lashed through the air, while a black mist lingered over the corpses of two boys, savoring their final moments.

Hicks was hanging in the air, held by a thick appendage wrapped tightly around his middle. Blood pouring down his body dripped off the toes of his leather shoes. His eyes were missing, and the skin of his face rippled like an ocean's current stirred from below. A sharp crack of bone further screwed up his skull. Then the meat over his cheeks unzipped as his mouth was pried open to an impossible angle, the jaw unplugging and hanging limply from his maw. Long fingers reached out from within the young man's mouth as the creature struggled to free itself from the orifice. The violent cracking sound of bones breaking snapped in the air. Hicks's skull burst, his shattered cranium cleaving apart the covering flesh, then his nose split in half as his whole head came apart.

A large, spidery, albino creature emerged from the gore. It shimmied down Hicks's chin to his shoulder. The thing was larger than any spider Hereford had ever seen, and its obscenely large abdomen sat upon more than a dozen appendages that resembled hands more than legs. Each long, multi-knuckled phalange ended in a sharp-looking point surrounded by bristling hairs. The sight reminded him instantly of a multi-pronged fishing spear. Its enormous mandibles were hooked, with jagged edges. Its eyes, like a collection of burning coal embers, were hot black fused with red lines. Behind it came its small children. Hundreds of them climbed from the pulpy soup of bone, tattered skin, and blood. The babies feasted, and they grew.

The air shrieked. A flurry of thin pages torn from the *Al Azif* whipped past his head. Bayley read still, his voice growing hoarse… and, Hereford noted, slightly panicked. The man's black magic had summoned far more than any of the plague cultists had bargained for.

More tendrils shattered the space of reality, lunging forth through the thinnies abridging their separate dimensions. Hereford stepped back from what appeared to be an oversized, empurpled palpus covered in thick saw-toothed antennae as it pushed through the window of its reality and into his own. What emerged was an enormous conglomeration of insectile anatomy overlaid upon spiny crustacean features. It slinked forward on a hundred legs, thousands of spiky nails sticking upward from the ribs of its piebald back and skull, its carapace a ruddy brown and sickly, spotted yellow. A trio of antennules probed the air ahead of its massive, segmented body, brushing against Douglas Quick's overcoat.

Hereford tripped over his feet as he maneuvered out of the way. His heels kicked at the slick floor, sliding uselessly as his shoes dug a trench through an odd mucus-like gruel.

The front-most segment of the crustacean rose, and long pointed limbs unfolded from beneath its wicked, clicking mandibles. It speared Quick through the shoulders, pinning the man's howling, writhing body to the floor. Quick's screams were mutilated into nightmarish noise then halted with a wet, gristly snap as the monster gorged.

Pounding and the noise of men clamoring came from the operating theater's entrance. The doors shuddered beneath angry fists and axes, then they snapped away from their frame in an explosion of wood. A dozen men fell into the room, nearly trampled by a dozen more pouring inside. And then those angry, sweat-covered faces absorbed the scene before them, halting in their tracks. Surprise and fright replaced the looks of hatred in their eyes. The front line turned on their heels, plowing into the men behind them, who, ignorant of what lay ahead, foiled their attempts at escape. The mob surged into the room, blind and deaf, seized entirely by a crazed ambition for revenge.

The albino arachnid-like horrors, having reduced

Hicks to little more than skeletal remains, scurried toward the mob, fueled solely by carnal appetites. Wave upon wave of monsters met men, washing over them, crawling atop one another in their pursuit of additional feasts.

Tentacles, lingering in the air from points unknown, lashed out, grabbing rioters off their feet and seizing them in powerful grips. Men were hoisted into the air, slammed into the ceiling, then pummeled upon the floor hard enough to split open skulls. Other tentacles competed to seize one body, pulling him in opposite directions. As if set upon a rack, the man's spine stretched and popped, his knees yanked loose of their sockets. His screams were lost in the wind, but the sight of his belly tearing open to spill his innards in a wet slop against the ground was not. His spine was torn free as his hips broke loose of the flesh and sinew supporting them, and his hollowed-out trunk sank in upon itself.

Men, and even a few women, Hereford saw, battled with shovels, picks, and axes, but such heroics were lost in the maelstrom of fear and madness. Propped against the wall, he watched the violence unfold and spread before him through the darkened glass lens of the plague mask. His clothes were sopped in a warm, unnatural liquid, but he paid it no mind. He was lost and enraptured, giddy with the madness of it all, even as his body shook with terror.

Bayley had stopped reading and was, in fact, no longer in the room at all. Hereford didn't care, though; he laughed, instead, at the absurdity of it all. He redirected his focus on the mayhem at the fore of the room, where pointed feelers impaled men and hell's own gods feasted upon flesh. The caged hearts beat faster and faster, thick strings of crackling electricity snapping across them and rising up and around the voltaic piles, casting the room in an erratic blue glow.

The words of Abd al-Hazred were true, truer than he ever could have imagined. And it was beautiful.

Hawley shoved through the crowd lingering on the fringes of New York Hospital. Inside, the riot was in full bloom, and although he could not see the activity within, he could hear quite well the bloodcurdling screams and demands for escape.

The mob, he thought, lost in a fugue of anger were tearing the doctors apart, exacting their street justice. He could imagine what grisly actions the medical students had been in the act of executing when they were interrupted and laid siege upon. Thinking of Jeremiah and Scipio, and the total lack of care exhibited by the Common Council, Hawley found it difficult to feel any degree of sympathy for the anatomists and students of the physic inside the building. He, after all, had come with his own aim toward vengeance.

A cold rain pelted those gathered outside the hospital, and his wet hand moved inside his jacket as he pushed his way between the protestors mindlessly shouting in the yard. His shoulder hit a solid-looking White man as he maneuvered, and the man seized his arm in an instant. Taller than Hawley, the White man looked down into Salem's eyes, a flash of anger boiling there.

"Pardon," Hawley said, his own eyes steeled beneath the scrutiny.

The man's eyes followed the line of Hawley's arm to the butt of the Ketland brass-barrel pistol holstered beneath the free man's overcoat. Their eyes met again, and the White man nodded. An air of understanding passed between them, and the man released Hawley.

"Let him through," he urged his neighbors, and bodies shuffled aside to make Hawley's passage easier.

Salem nodded at the man curtly and proceeded through the yard unmolested. Gun in hand, he strode up the hospital's steps to the front entrance. A malingering force seemed to radiate from the building itself, and although the doors were open, he certainly did not feel invited.

Inside, the building was unnaturally dark, the candles situated along either side of the hallway extinguished in their sconces. A pall of black vapor, not exactly smoke but something far more malodorous, coiled through the air. Hawley did not choke on the fetid musky stink so much as he gagged in revulsion.

A calamity of screams echoed down the corridor. Through the murky mist, he caught flashes of movement, but only just. He used his free hand to remove the tomahawk at his hip, feeling only slightly more secure with both his weapons at the ready.

Another scream, more a howling, then a piercing cry of torment reached his ears and was ended as quickly as it had begun. He hurried toward the far end of the corridor, heart hammering against his ribs as he recalled the screams on a hazy battlefield where a thick fog of gun smoke and black cannon powder had clouded the air.

Nearing the source of the agonized wailing, Salem Hawley saw a battlefield unlike any other. Pure white creatures with an unnatural assemblage of furred legs encircled a man in webbing. The webbing itself was caustic, and the smell of burning flesh assaulted Hawley's senses.

The webbing melted through skin, right down to the bone as it cut thin grooves all along the victim's body. One eye ruptured, and a thick goop popped from the eye socket to run down a ruined face. The insectile creature's netting soon dissolved through the entrapped man's neck, burning through vein and blood. His head canted at an impossible angle before he finally slumped and fell, dead and diced into an assortment of puzzle-like pieces.

Various horrifying scenes played out across a dozen other bodies, the hallway itself a mass grave. One figure clawed at his own face, digging fingers into his eyes, forcing them out of their sockets, and plunged his fingers into the bleeding craters, heedless of the pain. He ran straight into the wall, hands flat against the stained wallpaper, and beat his skull against it, over and over and over, screaming all the while.

Hawley then saw what had driven the man into such a craze—long, hairy fingers jutted free from *within* the man's ear canals. The skin all around the ear blistered and bulged outward until, finally, the flesh tore and the monster within found its freedom. Bony crunches followed as the man split his skull open, then more multi-legged, multi-segmented albino monstrosities poured free.

Hawley raised his pistol and fired. One of the albino creatures exploded, leaving behind a greenish, milky residue. Although he had a number of paper cartridges tucked into an inner pocket, to keep safe from the rain, he had no time to reload the single-shot flintlock. He swung the tomahawk at the approaching arachnids. Their attention firmly glued to him, they leapt toward him, and he swung again, the blade cutting through their soft skin, as he was forced back, already on his heels.

Shouting came from around him as some of the rioters sought to create order amid the chaos, demanding attention and giving orders as they swung their shovels or axes at the unnatural offenders. Hawley's back hit a door just as one of the spidery abominations sprang at his face. He dodged out of the way. The creature scrabbled against the wood door, aiming itself, again, at Hawley. Quickly, he buried his blade in the spider's midsection, cutting it squarely in half. He secured the flintlock in its leather holster beneath his coat then opened the door to create more space for maneuvering and fighting. The hallway had become logjammed with opposing forces, the air thick with that devilish vapor and filth besides.

The room he found himself in, however, contained its own share of horrid displays. Naked corpses were arrayed on several tables, butchered in various methods and manners. A man's sex organs had been pinned on the opposite wall, from the pelt of pubic hair to the flaccid cock withered against the sagging scrotum. Hawley gasped at the anatomical teaching display then put his back to it, turning his attention to the hallway once again.

More spider things were driving back the mob, dozens of them latching onto fleeing bodies and working in tandem to encase them in scorching, blistering gossamer. Hawley hurriedly tore open a paper cartridge with his teeth then set about reloading the flintlock. With the flashpan half full of powder, he closed the frizzen, poured the rest of the powder down the muzzle, and stuffed in the cartridge. He afforded himself a glance at the hallway as his hands worked, quickly removing the ramrod to stuff the ball and cartridge all the way to the breech, then replaced the ramrod. Time was of the essence against the fast-moving horrors, and he needed to keep the pistol ready for use. He holstered it, intending to save his one shot for when it was well and truly needed, and hurried back into the fray.

A woman cried out, red-faced as she beat at the ground with the back of her shovel blade. She pulled back, milky green gore dripping from the tool, and hammered it back down on another approaching wave. She swore, stomping to crush the smaller bugs beneath her shoes.

Hawley cut through another line of those jumping creatures, watching in horror as their brethren took down one more man. They bit into skin then burrowed into the opening. Bubbles rose across his flesh as they dug through his insides. Hawley rushed forward, hatchet raised to finish the man's suffering and—

He froze, his mind unable to comprehend what lay ahead. A score of tentacles danced in the air, attached to no physical form and without beginning, grabbing a hold of anybody that dared too close, or impaling them with hooked points at the end of their feelers.

A massive alien creature stalked forward on an impossible number of legs, gore and thick drool dripping from its misshapen maw. Mandibles hinged open to reveal a tunnel of teeth and jagged spines, then the jaws clicked shut over the skull of some poor bastard attempting to hack at it with an axe. The creature rose, grabbing ahold of the rest of the man's body in its alien appendages. A pair of men leapt forward, axes in hand, and took their chances. The spined beast fell upon them, popping their bodies as if the men were little more than too-full blood leeches, then it roared.

Movement snapped Hawley's attention back to the immediate as the man directly before him fell to his knees, cradling his head in both hands. His screams were worse than anything Hawley had witnessed in war. More bugs exploded free of the man's cranium, spattering Hawley with blood, bone, and gristle. He saw, too clearly, small white bodies filling and writhing in the skull's various cavities. He hammered at them with the tomahawk, further destroying the man's head with each blow, and hoping to take out as many of the creatures as he could. As the bugs shook free of the body, he danced a nervous jig, squashing what he could. More feet danced around him, and he saw the sweating, red-faced woman grinding the bugs into the soiled floor beside him.

"We have to get out of here," she said, swiping a loose lock of soaked hair from her eyes.

"We need fire," Hawley said. "There must be something we can use."

"In the labs, perhaps?" she suggested.

He nodded at the door past her shoulder. "I'll check in there."

"I'll keep them at bay."

He thanked her as he passed, slamming through the door and into another macabre room. Skeletons lined the tables, the bones arranged neatly for study. He followed the smell of cooking meat to a large pot over the fire. A glance inside showed a head within the bubbling water, the skin boiling off the bone.

He tugged on a pair of nearby gloves, pulled the heavy pot free, and lugged it out of the room. "Watch out!" he shouted then tossed the pot, spilling scalding hot water across the floor. The waxy head rolled through the muck after it.

Better some burned feet than a horrid death, he thought.

The spidery bugs' squealing as they boiled to death brought Hawley a measure of satisfaction, even as he disregarded the baleful looks of the men caught in the assault. He had made no friends, certainly, but it was of little importance.

Already the woman was following with makeshift torches, swinging the flames toward the spiders and reducing them to cinders. The mob grew wise to the idea and began imitating her tactics.

The hallway grew ripe with the smoldering carcasses of the albino spiders. The fur of their legs smoked as the fat on their bodies popped and sizzled, the flames spreading. Smoke rose as more torches were flung in support of the men still engaged in melee combat against writhing tentacles and the massive, devouring spiny creature.

Hawley took up a torch and strode into the operating theater, stepping across corpses as he went. A muscly limb darted toward him, and he met it with fire. Burned, the feeler snapped away, and he swung at it with the tomahawk but did little more than chop into the thick meat. Leery of the other tentacles snapping through the air, searching and lusting for blood, he pressed his advantage, holding flame to pallid flesh. He buried the blade into the tentacle again, taking out a good bit of meat, and chopped at it again. Fire, blade, fire, blade. The tentacle coiled in upon itself and retreated. To where, Hawley had no idea. The limb had been there then gone. Other men went after other tentacles with axes, spears, and torches. Some stepped too close or grew too cocksure, and that was enough to spell their grisly end.

A flurry of snow blinded Hawley briefly, a thick swirl of white flakes obscuring the thick feelers around him. *Strange*, he thought for a moment, recalling the early-spring rain that had turned the skies gray. As the snow dissipated, he glanced toward the shattered windows at the fore of the operating theater. Its surrounding drapery burned like Roman candles as men took flame to the cloth. Beyond, though, the rain was still falling. In defiance of this fact, another cold gale wrapped its shivering fingers about him, whipping stinging snow into his eyes. Momentarily, he caught sight of a plague doctor slumped against the wall before a meaty vine snared the doctor about the waist, hauling him off the ground to hoist him high into the air. And then the limb disappeared through the swirling vortex it had emerged from, taking the plague doctor with it.

A bolt of blue lightning drew Hawley's eyes to the surface of the worktable the doctor had been hiding under. A trio of cages sizzled beneath the electric current, and he caught a whiff of burnt offal. The display was unnatural even in a hospital, of that he had no doubt. Like the actions of the resurrectionists, this odd construct of cages, batteries, and organs was an affront to God.

Hawley knew what must be done. In but a few long strides, he crossed the operating theater and stood before the table, his tomahawk held aloft. The electric discharge raised the hairs all over his body. Dead and blackened hearts beat with impossible strength, wrapped in coils of bright-blue electricity. He swung the blade, upending the cages and snapping loose the copper wires connecting them to the large battery. The hum of electricity died, and the inhuman screams grew louder in response.

Behind Hawley, the spiny crustacean roared—in pain, in anger, or in victory, Hawley did not know. He turned in time to see its bulk occlude the door, a small portion of its many legs jamming into the space between the frame. Hawley hacked at the legs, slashing above and below the knobby joints. A spray of hot gore splashed him, and where it touched his skin, he grew hot and itchy. His body tingled with a slight burn, and he stepped away from the beast.

An elbow cuffed his ear, and he turned to see a man in combat against the mysterious appendage piercing the void. The man had no awareness of his surroundings as he wildly swung his torch. Flames scalded the side of Salem's face, and he lurched away in pain before his hair caught on fire. His hand went to his cheek, the skin already blistered. Even despite the pain, one thought arose: *Do not linger here.* As he fled from the torch, he saw that the impossible window was beginning to close around the otherworldly tentacle. The field of stars behind it diminished until finally it snapped shut, winking out of existence. The disembodied limb fell to the ground with a heavy slap. All around them, the portals were beginning to close and vanish.

The floor groaned as the spiny crustacean moved, its bulk putting cracks in the wall as it lodged itself into the doorframe and attempted to breach hind end first. Barely enough room existed between creature and doorframe for Hawley to pass through, and soon, even that small opening would be gone. The beast let out an ear-rattling bleat, and Salem plowed through the gap, back into the hallway, and to the front of the creature. He prayed for an end to the nightmare.

Smoke wrapped his face, seared his nostrils. His vision was hazy as smoke drew tears from his eyes, and he coughed into the crook of his arm, his breathing ragged and pained. Like his face, his lungs felt on fire as he inhaled gritty air.

At the front of the beast, men clashed with reaching, insectile arms and dodged a lunging, snapping mouth. Hawley put his tomahawk to work in their aid, parrying with the torch. One of the creature's antennae swung toward him, and he took the blade to it, deftly slicing the thin stalk away from the animal's head. It screamed, its hot breath a gust stinking of rotten meat. Even over the thick fumes of smoke, the stench immediately turned Hawley's stomach. The creature lunged forward, and

Hawley was barely able to roll out of the way in time. The hallway shook as the monstrosity dislodged its rear from the doorway. Its fore end stabbed toward where Salem had been but a moment ago, but it found only air.

The hospital was growing increasingly hot as the flames spread, and he knew the job had to be finished quickly, or it would be the end for all of them. He jammed the torch into the beast's gaping maw, where it caught on a long row of pointed spines lining the creature's gullet. Then he pulled the pistol.

He had only one shot. He raised the pistol, took aim, and—a body collided with him, knocking him off his feet. Both men hit the ground hard, and it took little imagining to realize the man had been flung out of the operating theater by one of those powerful feelers. The distraction was all the spiny monstrosity needed, and it turned toward them.

The monster's front segment reared up, the jagged hooks of its forelimbs snapping out into the air and stabbing downward to impale the man, along with Hawley, who was beneath him. Both were dragged off the floor, and for a moment, they hung suspended in the air. The pointed limb had run neatly through the man's spine and bore deeply into Hawley's belly, where it burned with sufficient agony. He could feel the life leeching away from him, even as he raised the tomahawk and brought it down upon the forelimb, hacking away at it with fading strength.

The crustacean screamed, its very presence foul and malignant. With consciousness dimming, Hawley surrendered the tomahawk and held the smooth-bore pistol before him. He rotated the flintlock's cock to full-cock and released the safety lock, then he leveled the gun at the alien horror. Hawley steadied his aim by grasping his wrist in the opposite hand, using the dead man's shoulder before him to help support his weakening arm, and pulled the trigger. Flint struck the frizzen, and a shower of sparks exploded across the flashpan. Past the brass barrel, one of the crustacean's eyes burst, ejecting a geyser of fluid from its orbit.

Below, a set of men hacked at the monster's underbelly, stabbing it with fishing spears or chopping at the thin layer of exposed skin with axes, shovel blades, or meat hooks. A rifle sounded then the ball blasted a small hole into the creature, just beneath its parted, seeking mandibles. The rifleman soon followed, the attached bayonet sinking into flesh and cutting upward.

Scipio! The man's presence flooded Hawley with relief. Abbie had done him well, and for that, he was grateful.

Organs pressed against the openings slashed into the creature's underside. Then intestines sloughed through and spilled to the wooden floor with a bloody smack and a noxious stench. The creature screamed, rearing back farther, unsettling its innards all the more. It hit the ground with a building-shaking crash, and Hawley was tossed free of the thing's forelimb. Air burst from his lungs, and as he inhaled, he got another mouthful of choking smoke.

Hands found him, and his eyes jolted open to see Scipio's stern face studying him.

"Thank God," the older man said. He put pressure on Hawley's belly, and Salem winced at the pain. "Can you move?"

"With help, I think."

Scipio nodded and got one of Hawley's arms around his shoulder, then he helped Hawley to his feet. "Keep a hand on your gut. Press down real hard."

"I will," Hawley said. A perverse thought rolled through his mind. *If only there were a doctor around.* If not for the pain, he might have laughed.

Jonathan Hereford recalled the strokes of heat singeing his flesh, but it was the lashes of painfully freezing cold that awoke him. His hands sank into the snow up to his wrists, his fingers hitting the hard, unyielding surface of ice beneath. The cold was so sudden and severe that it burned his skin. His teeth clattered uncontrollably and with such violent force, he worried they would break apart. He rolled to his knees, sinking into the achingly sharp bed of snow, and struggled to his feet. His hands were numb and had turned a scarlet red. The fingers took too long to respond as he demanded them to curl into a fist before burying them in the pockets of his leather overcoat. In one pocket, his fingers struck something hard and metallic—the handle of a scalpel. He held the blade in his hand, winning a small sense of security from the instrument.

Looking around, he saw nothing but a freezing white expanse. The wind howled, and he was momentarily grateful for the beaked mask he wore, although the cold penetrated even that. He was not dressed nearly properly enough for such savage elements, and he knew neither where to go nor where he even truly was. All around him was white, crisp and pure. Even the sky was a muted grayish white, and the horizon and the earth blended into a solid wall of murky off-white.

He stumbled forward, already unable to feel his toes, sinking up to his calves in fresh powder. A harsh gale cut through the smoked glass lenses of his mask, stabbing at his face through the stitching and drawing tears from his eyes. He blinked them away before they could freeze, and even that simple movement seemed an exercise in will.

Slowly, he put one foot in front of the other, hauling his legs from the piling snow and forcing his boot to sink back in one step ahead. *Move or die.* Such were his only options, he realized.

Snow encircled him, thick sheets of it driving through the sky to pummel him. He kept his head lowered against the hard wind, shivering all the while, but occasionally, he raised his eyes to survey his progress, hoping against all of the ill fates in store for him that there was some sign of progress, some landmark he could navigate toward. All he saw was white and white turning to a soft gray.

His gums and jaw ached from his teeth knocking against one another. With each step, his fear mounted, and his unfeeling body froze ever deeper, right down to his core. Still, he walked, preferring to die on his feet rather than on his back.

The more he puzzled over the issues of where he was and how he had gotten there, the more fleeting the answers became. He recalled the flames, the beating of dead hearts, and the shimmering of thinnies just at the edges of his vision. Then the reaching grasp of large, muscular limbs growing toward him from the unknown began to crystallize. The deeper he pushed into the freezing hellscape before him, the more he began to recall of those searching tentacles seizing bodies around him and of the Negro wielding the weapon of a native savage. Their eyes had met ever so briefly. Hereford had loomed over the Negro from an impossible height.

Hereford remember being suspended in the air, then the heat had simply vanished. He had been grabbed up by one of those tentacles, and the oxygen had been sucked from his lungs as he was pulled through the thinnie and into… not here, he knew. This arctic nightmare had merely been the endpoint of his travels. There had been something in between his abduction from the hospital and his delivery in the snow.

He could very nearly feel the heat of his body leeching away, as if it had been given form and flight. Beneath the beaked mask, tears were frozen to his cheeks and the pools of moisture over his eyes had turned to ice. He could no longer blink, and beneath those chips of ice, his vision burned.

He knew not how long he had been walking, and the path of his progress was already buried under fresh snow. It was impossible to tell even how far he had come, but he continued on nonetheless. Forward, always forward.

A swirl of snow cut across his vision, blinding him. Through the thickness, at the corner of his quite limited vision, he saw a shape, ever so briefly. Hereford worried it was only an illusion, a mirage of his own imagining. But as the snow drove upon him, harder and harder, he turned toward that new point, and he saw that, yes, something was there. Though indistinct and formless due to distance and his own blurred sight, it was certainly real enough. The shape was a dark smudge on the horizon, darker than the deepening gray of the sky as night fell.

Laughter escaped his aching, split lips.

When night came, even the darkness did little to cut away the shifting white void. The sky merely darkened to a lesser, murkier white, but still, white it remained. The shape, somehow no closer, was merely a form darker than the darkness surrounding it.

Howling wind slammed into him, tossing Hereford's hunched form off his feet. He crashed through the powdery top layer of snow and hit the ice hard, what little air he had in his lungs gushing out of him. Cold seeped into his bones during the moment it took him to recover. His body refused to move, his limbs frozen stiff, his will sapped entirely. As he found his knees, another ferocious wind blew into him, seizing his beaked mask in its grip and hauling it off his head.

"No," he gasped, hard chips of snow nipping at his frozen cheeks.

He prayed that his death would come quickly. Then, in a flash of insight, he recalled the scalpel in his pocket and thought of dyeing the snow around him red with his slashed wrists or perhaps his opened throat. If he could maintain a firm enough grip on the blade, he was so numb, he wouldn't even feel the pain of suicide. Even at that, his mind rebelled, and he hoarsely whispered, "No," once more. Although he wanted to sob, his eyes were crusted open, the tear ducts sealed by ice. In the unending tornado of white, he caught sight of the black shape, off in the distance, across an impossible void. Still, it was an encouragement, enough to give him some small measure of hope, a sliver to cling to as he forced his way back to his stiffened feet.

Hereford marched on, as unyielding as the harsh clime around him, as unfeeling as his body had become. Even his sweat had frozen, gluing his hair to his scalp in uneven, twisted furrows shaped by the wind, not unlike the arctic ridges and hillocks he stumbled across and through.

He swore he had made no progress, as the black point remained out of reach, a consistent blur off in the distance. He was wrought with such craven despair that he could no longer even scream, his mouth crusted shut by frozen snot and spittle.

"Let me die," he whispered. God, Elder or otherwise,

116 Michael Patrick Hicks

refused to listen as he trudged onward.

Overcome by weakness and desperation, he collapsed. The snow buried his numb body. The world had become divided, cut in half by pure white and empty pitch, the stars lost among the snow.

Still, some small ember of hope burned within him, despite his plea for death. Or perhaps it was the unquenchable curiosity that had defined so much of his life, the curiosity that had, ultimately, left him stranded in this frozen land. He was weak and exhausted, and yet he sought some answer to the hows and whys of his current predicament. He needed answers, and the more rational part of his mind insisted he would not find those by lying here in the snow waiting to die.

He raised his hand, intending to rise once more—one last time, perhaps—and struck something solid. Beneath a wall of snow, given form by the structure it had buried, was a smooth plane of ice. His hand stuck fast to it, and he had to pull hard to free himself. Skin tore off, leaving his palm an angry, wounded red. He'd barely felt the tug of flesh pulling loose. The combination of adrenaline over his discovery and the freezing numbness encasing his whole form created a deadly brotherhood.

Cradling his bleeding hand against his belly, he followed the line of the black wall, up and up and up, to a point far overhead. The wall was sheer, even as it angled smoothly toward the heavens.

A pyramid! A nervous titter blossomed in his chest, choked down by a far more nervous coughing that painfully twisted the meat of his lungs.

He set out, intending to circle the massive structure, a feeling of awe suddenly making him forget his desire for death and the torment of his body. Hewing close to the wall, he set about the perimeter of the pyramid, seeking an entrance but finding only a smooth, flat surface.

There has to be a way inside, he thought, notes of panic creeping into his thoughts. His heart raced, what little calm he had left escaping him entirely.

Wind lashed at him, encircling him in a crazed gust to beat him from all sides. And in that arctic fury, he saw powder wicked away from the looming wall beside him, a minor avalanche tumbling down the surface and falling neatly away. Revealed before him was a small indentation, a hollow of sorts, and he reached toward it. The snow was packed, thick and hard, but he pried at it with blackened fingers, hauling it away a fistful at a time. The hollow grew larger, until he was digging at a hole proper, laughing madly at himself the deeper he tunneled.

He dug a mouth just wide enough to crawl into, then his fingers broke through the wall of snow, touching warm air on the other side. He punched at the edges of snow until his knuckles split and bled, until he had created a gap large enough to shoulder through. He drove himself deeper into the hole, the weight of the snow pressing down against his back and ribs, squeezing him like a tentacle and pressing the air out of him. His boots kicked at the earth, driving him forward, propelling him through the crusty, freezing wall. The crown of his skull broke through, and as he pushed farther in, he saw before him only darkness. The dry air felt only slightly warmer than the inhospitable elements outside. But the discovery alone was enough to invigorate him, and he hurried inside.

The corridor he found himself in was long and dark, and it offered but one direction. He had no choice but to follow it, as it slowly widened and opened into a hollow, massive chamber.

Inexplicably, fire warmed the arena, torches burned brightly in their sconces mounted along the walls. More burst into life, scores of them, hundreds of them. And what the light revealed made Hereford scream.

Chapter 8

The day's first movements drew a pained wince from Salem Hawley. His arm promptly went to his wounded belly, cradling it as he propped himself up on one elbow. He didn't recognize the small, simply decorated room, and it took a moment for his sleep-addled brain to catch up. He pushed himself farther into a sitting position then rested his back against the headboard before taking a long moment to recover from the exertion. His side ached, and a fresh, hot wetness bloomed to darken the already-stained bandages encircling his abdomen. He had given serious thought to standing but quickly reconsidered.

A pitcher of water, along with a filled glass, had been left on the nightstand. Beside it was a leather-bound copy of a book written by James Cook, *A Voyage Toward the South Pole*. Hawley decided to whittle away the time with a chapter or two while his body reinvigorated itself.

After but a few pages into Cook's account, a knock sounded on the door, and Scipio poked his head through. Smiling companionably, he pushed the door open farther, a small tray of tea in hand. "I honestly wasn't sure if you would be awake."

Hawley took a draught from the water glass. "Oh, I'm awake, but I honestly don't feel much like moving."

Scipio laughed, placing the tea set atop the dresser, then moved to the neighboring window and pulled apart the drapes. The sheer brightness of the sunlight blinded Hawley, and he had to raise a forearm before his eyes to see properly.

After a grunt, Scipio pulled the drape back far enough to blot out the sun while still leaving the room bright and cheery. "Suppose we can close that up a bit, eh?"

"How long have I been out?"

"Better part of a day." Scipio prepared a cup of tea for each of them then took a seat opposite the bed, coolly studying Hawley. "City's still in chaos, riots all up and down Manhattan. Last I heard, there were eight dead."

"The creatures?"

"The creatures, yes, but men, too. It seems that those… well, those *things*, have been dealt with. They were concentrated at the hospital, and apparently, fire is a fairly natural deterrent for their kind. Depending on the tongues wagging, pray tell you hear of an ungodly spider or few having been dealt with, but with the hospital up in flames, it appears we can draw that particular chapter to a close. Protests against the experts of the physic continue unabated, however, and quite violently at that."

"And of the doctors? What of them? The ones who drew all this madness forth?"

Scipio sipped at his tea. "A number of doctors staffed at the hospital have been rounded up and jailed, but largely for their safety more than anything else. To *protect* them."

Hawley clicked his tongue against the roof of his mouth then shook his head.

"One will be arriving here soon, in fact, to survey your wounds. I did the best I could, but a professional's eye is needed."

"Is it bad?" Hawley asked.

Scipio shrugged. "I've seen worse. I dare say we have both seen much worse, but I'm not a doctor. A professional's eye shouldn't hurt."

Hawley set his cup aside then sank back into the pillow. If he listened carefully, he could hear the calamity of a city ensconced in its own destruction and the occasional faint boom of gunfire.

"Damn it all," he muttered, his belly throbbing painfully. Listening to the dim clinking of a teacup settling upon a plate and the soft sips of the older man drinking, he slipped softly back into the embrace of exhaustion.

Richard Bayley's stagecoach drew to the door of the freed man's home, Scipio as he recalled. It was fitting, he supposed, that he should treat the companion of the man whom John Hicks, Jr. had assaulted on his way to absconding with a body planted in the freed black's graveyard. So fitting, in fact, that Bayley could not help but smile. Even that simple act, though, aggravated the oversized knot on his skull, but still, he wondered at the cyclical nature of fate and the demands of the Elders.

He climbed the porch steps, his small black medical bag in hand, and delivered three hard raps to the wooden front door. A well-muscled, but clearly aged, Negro answered his summons, and they exchanged a brief introduction.

"He's through here," Scipio said, leading Bayley down a short hallway of his small, Spartan house. "May I offer you some tea?"

Bayley nodded, impressed by the man's politeness. Scipio clearly had some education to temper his savage instincts. Since the war, Bayley had been providing aid to Manhattan's poor, including the Negro population. This ruse provided him with ample means to carry out his experiments, while also keeping him free of suspicions that occasionally stemmed from his work, on those rare instances that his work was noticed. To the city's credit, it did not often notice a missing orphan, and whatever claims were sometimes—but rarely—made by the Negroes were easily dismissed. To his own credit, it was not often that he provided the unwitting souls he crossed paths with cause to complain. More often than not, he provided them with relief whenever possible and was very careful to choose an appropriate victim, such as the prostitutes he and his fellow plague doctors had been experimenting upon.

And my, how those experiments bore fruit! His face ached as he worked to keep his smile at bay. If he were forced to admit it, a small part of his mind, the one that had been honed by science and his studies of the natural world, had dismissed the promises stored within the pages of *Al Azif*. Such doubt was natural, of course, given the extreme and wild nature of the claims made within that tome. But these doubts were heavily overwhelmed by *belief*, as well as those ethereal creatures he had witnessed on the battlefield little more than a decade prior.

The magic contained in *Al Azif* was very real, indeed. *Perhaps a bit too real*, he thought ruefully. He had panicked, and even now, his own cowardice shamed him. He had summoned forth the Elders, and in what should have been a moment of awed worship, he had run, the primal part of his mind seizing control and forcing him to flee in terror.

"This is Salem Hawley," Scipio said, interrupting Bayley's thoughts. The freed man put his back to Bayley to pour tea, his shoulders hunched. Freed, yet still deferential.

I could take a blade to your throat and speak the words of offering, Bayley thought. *I could recall them here to this plane of existence and end all of you!* Instead, he said only, "Thank you," as he accepted the proffered cup of tea then sipped gingerly at it. "Mmm," he said, raising his eyebrows, somewhat surprised that the drink was actually quite well steeped.

Whether it was their few words spoken or their mere presence and movements that had woken him, Hawley began to stir. His eyelids fluttered then began to focus, pinning his gaze squarely on the doctor.

"Mr. Hawley, I am Dr. Bayley."

Bayley set his tea on the nearby table. He then placed his medical bag on the seat of a chair beside the bed. "May I examine your injury?"

Hawley nodded, watching the doctor carefully as

his bedsheets were folded away with an uncommon gentleness. The bandages wrapped around his belly were stained the color of rust, and Bayley noticed a fair amount of spotting on the top sheet as it pulled stickily away from him.

"I don't know that I can pay you," Hawley said.

Bayley nodded, assessing the younger man before him. The black man's torso was puckered with scars. Some, he recognized as lash marks from a whip and suspected there were quite a number more along his backside. One hilled bit of scar tissue was quite plainly a bullet wound, and some of the slashes he believed to be knife marks or injuries from a bayonet.

"You fought in the rebellion?"

Hawley studied Bayley's expressionless face, perhaps considering the doctor's British lilt, then slowly nodded. "I did. On the colonial side." The tone of his voice was goading, but Bayley ignored it and set about cutting away the mess of bandages.

"And this wound? You were stabbed, run through?"

Hawley grimaced as Bayley pulled the bandages away from the wound. "Hm," was all he said, neither a confirmation nor a denial.

"At the hospital? During the riots, perhaps?"

Again, Hawley studied Bayley's face for a moment, clearly weighing potential responses. After a moment, he nodded. "That's right."

Bayley leaned close to the wound. The hole appeared smooth enough, and whatever had lanced the man had gone through cleanly. He applied some force to the man's hip, encouraging him to turn on his shoulder so he could see the opposite side.

Turning to Scipio, he said, "Bring me some washcloths, water, and a candle, please." Then, back to Hawley, he said, "I will give you a tincture for the pain, and I will stitch the openings shut. Keep it clean and be careful not to tax yourself, and I believe you will make a full recovery."

"That's it, huh?"

Bayley smiled. "What else need there be?"

He took a seat beside Hawley and drew the chair in close. He wiped away the dried blood with a wet rag, carefully exposing the edges of raw, ruined flesh. The wound seeped, but not unexpectedly so. He turned to expose a sewing needle to the candle's flame then offered Hawley a stick to bite. "This will hurt, I'm afraid."

Hawley laughed mirthlessly. "I've been stitched before. Felt worse before too."

"A few drops of this then." Bayley removed a tonic from his bag and gave Hawley an eyedropper filled with golden fluid. "Five drops should suffice."

Hawley eyed the dropper skeptically, as he would any tonic given to him by a strange white man, regardless of his profession. Bayley, unfortunately, wasn't intent on administering further treatments until Hawley had taken the drug, so Hawley capitulated. He placed the eyedropper in his mouth and squeezed out five drops.

Satisfied, Bayley drew the needle and thread through the wound's edge then said, "What did you see at the hospital?"

The former slave, his face screwed up in pain, gave him a baleful glance. "Viciousness. Evil. And more death than was needed."

"The rumors..." Bayley let his voice trail off then shrugged as if thinking better of what he had been about to say. He turned a raised eye to Hawley, who nodded for him to continue. "There were, well, that is to say, there are rumors of monsters. Ridiculousness, I should think."

Hawley continued to watch the doctor's stitching, and Bayley occasionally looked up toward his patient.

As he sewed the gory circle together, taking more time than was truly needed, he saw the black man's eyes waver as he struggled to focus through the fog of the tincture.

"Not so ridiculous," Hawley said, at last. "There were monsters indeed, like nothing of this earth."

"There is a book, you know," Bayley said softly. "A book of spells, of magic. Otherworldly, powerful magic." He added hastily, "More rumors, perhaps. You know how rumors are."

"And what do these rumors suggest?" Hawley asked, a keen note of interest in his slurred voice.

"You're aware of these grave robberies, I trust? Of course, how could you not be? And the riots all across the city? These things are connected. You were there. You saw what happened, yes?"

"Yes," Hawley said, his voice weakening.

"There are rumors within the medical community that these rogue scholars were performing a dark séance of sorts, and that was what had caused all of this commotion. If what you say is true, about these monsters, that is, then perhaps there is some credence to these rumors."

Hawley's mouth hung open, his slack tongue protruding from his mouth. Bayley hoped that he had not overplayed his hand nor that the man was too drugged out of his mind to seize the opportunity to come.

"Several of my colleagues have fled the city or have otherwise disappeared as a result of yesterday's commotion. One of them, I suspect, has this book."

"Where?" Hawley asked, his eyes fighting to focus on the doctor. The single word came out slowly and thickly, his eyes glassy.

"Northeast of here, in Massachusetts, most likely."

The men were quiet for a beat as Bayley finished stitching the anterior side of the injury. After a suitable amount of time elapsed, Bayley continued. "You had mentioned the issue of payment. I will make you an offer, and if you agree, then we can consider that matter closed. I want you to retrieve this book and return it to me."

"Why... w... would you want... it?"

Bayley paused in his work to meet the man's eye. He put an edge of steel in his voice, a hint of anger that he did not truly feel. "To destroy it. You've seen what that book is capable of, what men in wrongful possession of it are capable of. The city may be calming now, but less than twenty-four hours ago, it was a tinderbox, all because of that damnable book and the rogues handling it. After what you've witnessed, could you rest easy knowing it is still out there?"

For a long moment, Hawley studied the doctor's face, his eyes struggling to focus. Yet his intent was so studious, Bayley wondered if the man possessed some arcane vision to see into his very soul and know that he was lying. And then his patient blinked languorously and nodded, reaching a decision through the fog of pain and tincture.

"I'll get you... this book," he slurred. "And we'll... we'll destroy it... together."

"Then, I fear it may be I who will be in your debt, sir."

Bayley set aside his needle and thread and held his hand before Hawley. They shook, their agreement sealed.

"Now, onto your side, Mr. Hawley, so that I may finish."

Once Bayley had settled into the leather seat of his stagecoach and the driver had set the horses forth, he withdrew a small tonic from his medical bag. A fierce headache was winding through his skull, enough to make him nauseous.

Damn that woman, he thought, his hand going to the stiff hill of skin rising atop the back of his head. Neither Post nor Dr. Heather Ellery had been intent on dying within the operating theater of New York Hospital, and along with Bayley, they had broken the nearest window to seek escape. He had cared little of the fates of Hicks, Quick, or Hereford as he abandoned his plague garments and lit upon the yard surrounding the hospital, heading into the woods beyond.

Once they were a safe enough distance away, that sniveling cunt had lashed out at him from behind, slamming a cudgel into his skull. He had dropped to his knees instantly, the grimoire fumbling free of his grip. With surprising viciousness, she'd turned quickly on her heel and slammed her cudgel into Post's face numerous times, until the man went still. She'd left him alive, yes, but badly beaten and unconscious. Bayley had been too dazed to do little more than watch through blurry eyes as Ellery seized *Al Azif* from him, and then he was lost to the shadows as the woman disappeared.

After wakening and making their way out of the woods, convincing the watchmen to afford them protection from further assaults by rioters had been a simple task. Lying overnight in a jail cell, unable to sleep comfortably, he'd vowed to get that book back.

Ellery, he knew, had come to Manhattan from the Essex County region of Massachusetts. She still had family there, and after a search of her apartment earlier that morning, he'd surmised she would return to Essex

County. Her Manhattan flat had been empty, clothes strewn about carelessly. Jewelry and other personal effects were missing. Her neighbors had confirmed that she had indeed left, in quite a hurry, to parts unknown.

The book would be his, and Ellery would be damned for her thievery, her betrayal, and blind ambitions. His only regret was the delay required while Hawley recovered. The Negro owed him a debt now, and Hawley would follow through. If the freed man failed, though, he would not be missed. Not like Bayley or Post, who could not simply up and disappear without raising more than a few eyebrows and perhaps even the curiosity of the law.

He eased back into the cushions, the tonic soothing his burdens. He barely even noticed the carriage's jostling as it bumped along the pitted path toward his home. Relaxing, he smiled, wondering again at the hands of fate and the destiny of the Elders.

He would have his grimoire returned to him. Then, he would be free to begin again. He would see to it that the Elders turned their attention toward this world and that this world, in turn, would burn. His gods would come forth with their rule of agony and suffering, and it would be beautiful.

Salem Hawley Will Return in
Borne of the Deep

Coming soon…

A note to readers

Thank you for choosing to read my work – it is greatly appreciated and I hope you enjoyed the journey.

If you would be willing to spare a minute or two, please leave a brief review of this work and let other readers know what you thought. Reviews are incredibly helpful, particularly for an independent author and publisher such as myself, and can help determine the success of a novel. Reviews do not need to be long – twenty words or so should suffice – but their impact can be enormous.

I look forward to your thoughts, and thank you, once again, for taking the time to read this story.

If you would like to know about upcoming releases, I encourage you to subscribe to my newsletter at http://michaelpatrickhicks.com.

Acknowledgements

I began writing this book, and the Salem Hawley series as a whole, in February of 2017, shortly after listening to the audiobook version of *Stiff: The Curious Lives of Human Cadavers* by Mary Roach. At some point in that book, she briefly mentioned the topic of resurrectionists, medical students and anatomists who dug up and stole the corpses of the recently dead. I began to get a little tickle of an idea in the back of my head and took to the great Google machine.

Now, I don't remember if Roach discussed this in her book or if it was a topic that came up in the course of my research, but as my story ideas grew, I knew that the crux of this first novella would hinge on the New York Doctors' Riot of 1788.

I set about learning as much as I could about the Doctors' Riot and set about portraying it with plenty of authorial license. Yes, I admit, dear readers, the *actual* Doctors' Riot did not feature any otherworldly monstrosities, and the cultists were the product of my own imagination, even if I borrowed some degree of their likenesses from the historical record. I also fudged the invention of the voltaic pile, the experiments of which were hypothesized, tested, and published by Alessandro Volta in 1791. The creation of the voltaic pile as depicted here would not come from Volta until 1800. For the sake of this story, I made Volta's publications come about a few years earlier and allowed Dr. Bayley to devise its construction in secret for his own devious purposes. If there are any electrical engineers and other associated sticklers for details, I can only ask for your forgiveness.

In the build-up toward this book's climax and various plot points along the way, I found Bess Lovejoy's 2014 article, "The Gory New York City Riot that Shaped American Medicine," for Smithsonian.com to be a wonderful starting point: https://www.smithsonianmag.com/history/gory-new-york-city-riot-shaped-american-medicine-180951766/

Other sources that proved invaluable along the way included the following:

- "The Doctors' Mob Riot" by Greg Bjerg for Damn Interesting. Retrieved from https://www.damninteresting.com/the-doctors-mob-riot/
- "American Resurrection: The Doctors' Riot of 1788" by Francesca Miller for Dirty, Sexy History. Retrieved from https://dirtysexyhistory.com/2016/07/07/american-resurrection-the-doctors-riot-of-1788/
- "Body Snatchers of Old New York" by Bess Lovejoy for Lapham's Quarterly. Retrieved from https://www.laphamsquarterly.org/roundtable/

body-snatchers-old-new-york
- "The Doctors' Riot 1788" by The History Box. Retrieved from http://thehistorybox.com/ny_city/riots/riots_article7a.htm
- "'And What Say the Living?' An Examination of Public Discussion of Anatomical Dissection Prior to the Doctors' Riot of 1788" by Carmen Niemeyer. (http://research.monm.edu/mjur/files/2015/04/MJUR2015-09-NiemeyerB.pdf).

Since I was using a real event, I decided at some point along the way to use the names of those who were involved, although my depiction of them here is largely fictional. Some characters, like John Hicks, Jr., are fictional representations based on anecdotes about them from the period in which they lived. For Hicks, in particular, some aspects of his behavior were drawn from incidents lodged in the historical record, specifically the instigating moments of the Doctors' Riot as described in Niemeyer's article referenced above.

I haven't found any evidence yet on whether or not he might be a distant relative of mine, but I can't entirely rule it out, as playing a grisly prank on children that sparks a riot certainly sounds like something one of my relatives would do. Although Hicks seemed to be quite the instigator and rabble-rouser, there's no evidence to indicate he was ever a cultist or murderer.

For that matter, there is no evidence Richard Bayley was, either. In fact, he seems like a fairly well-practiced doctor of his era and was responsible for several good deeds on behalf of the fledgling city of New York, including the development of the Quarantine Act and the opening of the Quarantine Grounds and Marine Hospital. He spent quite a lot of his career caring for the sick, the poor, and immigrants newly arrived to the shores of America. You can find a timeline of his life at http://blogs.shu.edu/mvdh/people/dr-richard-bayley/ should you wish to know more about the real man I have taken extraordinary liberties with in order to tell my little horror story. I likely owe quite an apology to his spirit for the things I've written here and in the stories to come.

Salem Hawley and Jonathan Hereford are both entirely fictitious, and any slandering of them is wholly imaginary on my part.

In addition to the authors of the above-referenced sources, a number of other individuals were responsible for helping this story shape up on its road to publication. Jessica Anderegg was responsible for reading this manuscript in its initial form and providing much-needed feedback on its content and development, pointing out areas of weakness and strength and suggesting ways to make this book better, stronger, and faster. I would also like to thank my editor, Stefanie Spangler Buswell, who provided a number of very helpful notes, weeded out any textual mistakes, and made my prose shine. Additional thanks to Luara Brooks, who proofread the final manuscript and pointed out plenty of other mistakes I either introduced or missed as this book's various drafts took shape.

Should we ever meet, I owe Kealan Patrick Burke a round or two or three of his drink of choice for his luscious cover art. He's arranged art for the last few books of mine and is again responsible for the stunning imagery of this title and the two Salem Hawley books to follow.

Of course, I also owe a hell of a lot to my wife and kids, for both their support and their patience.

And, most of all, I owe you, too, dear readers. You make the work worth it, and I thank you for reading. I hope I've made this book worth your time, and I look forward to us meeting again soon.

Until next time...

ABOUT THE AUTHOR

Michael Patrick Hicks is the author of B*roken Shells: A Subterranean Horror Novella, Mass Hysteria*, and the science fiction thriller *Convergence*. He is a member of the Horror Writers Association and the Great Lakes Association of Horror Writers.

In addition to his own works of original fiction, he has written for the online publications Audiobook Reviewer and Graphic Novel Reporter, and has previously worked as a freelance journalist and news photographer in Metro Detroit.

Michael lives in Michigan with his wife and two children. In between compulsively buying books and adding titles that he does not have time for to his Netflix queue, he is hard at work on his next story.

To stay up to date on Michael's latest releases, join his newsletter at: http://bit.ly/1H8slIg

For more books and updates on Michael's work, visit his website: http://michaelpatrickhicks.com

CHECK OUT THESE
OTHER TITLES FROM

HIGH FEVER
BOOKS

MICHAEL PATRICK HICKS

BROKEN
SHELLS

BROKEN SHELLS

Antoine DeWitt is a man down on his luck. Broke and recently fired, he knows the winning Money Carlo ticket that has landed in his mailbox from a car dealership is nothing more than a scam. The promise of five thousand dollars, though, is too tantalizing to ignore.

Jon Dangle is a keeper of secrets, many of which are buried deep beneath his dealership. He works hard to keep them hidden, but occasionally sacrifices are required, sacrifices who are penniless, desperate, and who will not be missed. Sacrifices exactly like DeWitt.

When Antoine steps foot on Dangle's car lot, it is with the hope of easy money. Instead, he finds himself trapped in a deep, dark hole, buried alive. If he is going to survive the nightmare ahead of him, if he has any chance of seeing his wife and child again, Antoine will have to do more than merely hope. He will have to fight his way back to the surface, and pray that Jon Dangle's secrets do not kill him first.

AVAILABLE IN PRINT, EBOOK, AND AUDIOBOOK

MASS
HYSTERIA

MICHAEL PATRICK HICKS

MASS HYSTERIA

It came from space...

Something virulent. Something evil. Something new. And it is infecting the town of Falls Breath.

Carried to Earth in a freak meteor shower, an alien virus has infected the animals. Pets and wildlife have turned rabid, attacking without warning. Dogs and cats terrorize their owners, while deer and wolves from the neighboring woods hunt in packs, stalking and killing their human prey without mercy.

As the town comes under siege, Lauren searches for her boyfriend, while her policeman father fights to restore some semblance of order against a threat unlike anything he has seen before. The Natural Order has been upended completely, and nowhere is safe.

...and it is spreading.

Soon, the city will find itself in the grips of mass hysteria.

To survive, humanity will have to fight tooth and nail.

REVOLVER

MICHAEL PATRICK HICKS

"A classic example of social science fiction"
David Wailing, Author of Auto

FOREWORD BY
LUCAS BALE

REVOLVER

The "stunning and harrowing" short story, originally published in the anthology No Way Home, is now available as a standalone release and features an all-new foreword written by award-winning science fiction author, Lucas Bale.

Cara Stone is a broken woman: penniless, homeless, and hopeless. When given the chance to appear on television, she jumps at the opportunity to win a minimum of $5,000 for her family.

The state-run, crowdfunded series, Revolver, has been established by the nation's moneyed elite to combat the increasing plight of class warfare.

There's never been a Revolver contestant quite like Cara before. The corporate states of America are hungry for blood, and she promises to deliver.

AVAILABLE NOW IN EBOOK AND AUDIOBOOK

"A sharp, crackling exploration of man's hubris and science gone wrong. This is Frankenstein for the new millennium."

HUNTER SHEA, author of We Are Always Watching and The Jersey Devil

MICHAEL PATRICK HICKS

BLACK SITE

BLACK SITE

FOR FANS OF H.P. LOVECRAFT AND ALIEN COMES A NEW WORK OF COSMIC TERROR!

Inside an abandoned mining station, in the depths of space, a team of scientists are seeking to unravel the secrets of humanity's origin. Using cutting-edge genetic cloning experiments, their discoveries take them down an unimaginable and frightening path as their latest creation proves to be far more than they had bargained for.

"A sharp, crackling exploration of man's hubris and science gone wrong. This is Frankenstein for the new millennium." — **Hunter Shea, author of We Are Always Watching and The Jersey Devil**

THE
MARQUE

MICHAEL PATRICK HICKS

THE MARQUE

The world has fallen beneath the rule of alien invaders. The remnants of humanity are divided into two camps: those who resist, and those serve.

Darrel Fines serves. He is a traitor, a turncoat who has betrayed his people, his wife, and most of all, himself. In this new world order, in which humanity is at the very bottom, Fines is a lawman for the violent and grotesque conquerors.

When the offspring of the Marque goes missing, Fines is charged with locating and recovering the alien. Caught in the crosshairs of a subdued worker's camp and the resistance cell that he was once allied with, Fines is forced to choose between a life of servility and a life of honor.

AVAILABLE NOW IN EBOOK

——

For more titles and news about future releases, visit www.michaelpatrickhicks.com and subscribe to the mailing list.